Niels Lyhne

Niels Lyhne

Jens Peter Jacobsen

Translated from the Danish by
Hanna Astrup Larsen

ÆGYPAN PRESS

1880
This text from the New York edition published by the American-
Scandinavian Foundation in 1919.
Jens Peter Jacobsen lived from 1847 until 1885.

Niels Lyhne
A publication of
ÆGYPAN PRESS

www.aegypan.com

Chapter I

She had the black, luminous eyes of the Blid family, with delicate, straight eyebrows; she had their boldly shaped nose, their strong chin, and full lips. The curious line of mingled pain and sensuousness about the corners of her mouth was likewise an inheritance from them, and so were the restless movements of her head. But her cheek was pale, her hair was soft as silk and was wound smoothly around her head.

Not so the Blids; their coloring was of roses and bronze. Their hair was rough and curly, heavy as a mane, and their full, deep, resonant voices bore out the tales told of their forefathers, whose noisy hunting parties, solemn morning prayers, and thousand and one amorous adventures were matters of family tradition.

Her voice was languid and colorless. I am describing her as she was at seventeen. A few years later, after she had been married, her voice gained fullness, her cheek took on a fresher tint, and her eye lost some of its luster, but seemed even larger and more intensely black.

At seventeen she did not at all resemble her brothers and sisters; nor was there any great intimacy between herself and her parents. The Blid family were practical folk who accepted things as they were; they did their work, slept their sleep, and never thought of demanding any diversions beyond the harvest home and three or four Christmas parties. They never passed through any religious experiences, but they would no more have dreamed of not rendering unto God what was God's than they would have neglected to pay their taxes. Therefore they said their evening prayers, went to church at Easter and Whitsun, sang their hymns on Christmas Eve, and partook of the Lord's Supper twice a year. They had no particular thirst for knowledge. As for their love of beauty, they were by no means insensible to the charm of little sentimental ditties, and when summer came with thick, luscious grass in the meadows and grain sprouting in broad fields, they would sometimes say to one another that this was a fine time for traveling about the country, but their natures had nothing of the poetic; beauty never stirred any raptures in them, and they were never visited by vague longings or daydreams.

Bartholine was not of their kind. She had no interest in the affairs of the fields and the stables, no taste for the dairy and the kitchen — none whatever.

She loved poetry.

She lived on poems, dreamed poems, and put her faith in them above everything else in the world. Parents, sisters and brothers, neighbors and friends — none of them ever said a word that was worth listening to. Their thoughts never rose above their land and their business; their eyes never sought anything beyond the conditions and affairs that were right before them.

But the poems! They teemed with new ideas and profound truths about life in the great outside world, where grief was black, and joy was red; they glowed with images, foamed and sparkled with rhythm and rhyme. They were all about young girls, and the girls were noble and beautiful — how noble and beautiful they never knew themselves. Their hearts and their love meant more than the wealth of all the earth; men bore them up in their hands, lifted them high in the sunshine of joy, honored and worshiped them, and were delighted to share with them their thoughts and plans, their triumphs and renown. They would even say that these same fortunate girls had inspired all the plans and achieved all the triumphs.

Why might not she herself be such a girl? They were thus and so — and they never knew it themselves. How was she to know what she really was? And the poets all said very plainly that this was life, and that it was not life to sit and sew, work about the house, and make stupid calls.

When all this was sifted down, it meant little beyond a slightly morbid desire to realize herself, a longing to find herself, which she had in common with many other young girls with talents a little above the ordinary. It was only a pity that there was not in her circle a single individual of sufficient distinction to give her the measure of her own powers. There was not even a kindred nature. So she came to look upon herself as something wonderful, unique, a sort of exotic plant that had grown in these ungentle climes and had barely strength enough to unfold its leaves; though in more genial warmth, under a more powerful sun, it might have shot up, straight and tall, with a gloriously rich and brilliant bloom. Such was the image of her real self that she carried in her mind. She dreamed a thousand dreams of those sunlit regions and was consumed with longing for this other and richer self, forgetting — what is so easily forgotten — that even the fairest dreams and the deepest longings do not add an inch to the stature of the human soul.

One fine day a suitor came to her.

Young Lyhne of Lönborggaard was the man, and he was the last male scion of a family whose members had for three generations been among the most distinguished people in the country. As burgomasters, revenue collectors, or royal commissioners, often rewarded with the title of councilor of justice, the Lyhnes in their maturer years had served king and country with diligence and honor. In their younger days they had traveled in France and Germany, and these trips, carefully planned and carried out with great thoroughness, had enriched their receptive minds with all the scenes of beauty and the knowledge of life that foreign lands had to offer. Nor were these years of travel pushed into the background, after their return, as mere reminiscences, like the memory of a feast after the last candle has burned down and the last note of music has died away. No, life in their homes was built on these years; the tastes awakened in this manner were not allowed to languish, but were nourished and developed by every means at their command. Rare copper plates, costly bronzes, German poetry, French juridical works, and French philosophy were everyday matters and common topics in the Lyhne households.

Their bearing had an old-fashioned ease, a courtly graciousness, which contrasted oddly with the heavy majesty and awkward pomposity of the other county families. Their speech was well rounded, delicately precise, a little marred, perhaps, by rhetorical affectation, yet it somehow went well with those large, broad figures with their domelike foreheads, their bushy hair growing far back on their temples, their calm, smiling eyes, and slightly aquiline noses. The lower part of the face was too heavy, however, the mouth too wide, and the lips much too full.

Young Lyhne showed all these physical traits, but more faintly, and, in the same manner, the family intelligence seemed to have grown weary in him. None of the mental problems of finer artistic enjoyments that he encountered stirred him to any zeal or desire whatsoever. He had simply striven with them in a painstaking effort which was never brightened by joy in feeling his own powers unfold or pride in finding them adequate. Mere satisfaction in a task accomplished was the only reward that came to him.

His estate, Lönborggaard, had been left him by an uncle who had recently died, and he had returned from the traditional trip abroad in order to take over the management. As the Blid family were the nearest neighbors of his own rank, and his uncle had been intimate with them, he called, met Bartholine, and fell in love with her.

That she should fall in love with him was almost a foregone conclusion.

Here at last was someone from the outside world, someone who had lived in great, distant cities, where forests of spires were etched on a sunlit sky, where the air was vibrant with chimes of bells, the pealing of organs, and the twanging of mandolins, while festal processions, resplendent with gold and colors, wound their way through broad streets; where marble mansions shone, where noble families flaunted bright escutcheons hung two by two over wide portals, while fans flashed, and veils fluttered over the sculptured vines of curving balconies. Here was one who had sojourned where victorious armies had tramped the roads, where tremendous battles had invested the names of villages and fields with immortal fame, where smoke rising from gypsy fires trailed over the leafy masses of the forest, where red ruins looked down from vine-wreathed hills into the smiling valley, while water surged over the mill-wheel, and cowbells tinkled as the herds came home over wide-arched bridges.

All these things he told about, not as the poems did, but in a matter-of-fact way, as familiarly as the people at home talked about the villages in their own county or the next parish. He talked of painters and poets, too, and sometimes he would laud to the skies a name that she had never even heard. He showed her their pictures and read their poems to her in the garden or on the hill where they could look out over the bright waters of the fjord and the brown, billowing heath. Love made him poetic; the view took on beauty, the clouds seemed like those drifting through the poems, and the trees were clothed in the leaves rustling so mournfully in the ballads.

Bartholine was happy; for her love enabled her to dissolve the twenty-four hours into a string of romantic episodes. It was romance when she went down the road to meet him; their meeting was romance, and so was their parting. It was romance when she stood on the hilltop in the light of the setting sun and waved one last farewell before going up to her quiet little chamber, wistfully happy, to give herself up to thoughts of him; and when she included his name in her evening prayer, that was romance, too.

She no longer felt the old vague desires and longings. The new life with its shifting moods gave her all she craved, and moreover her thoughts and ideas had been clarified through having someone to whom she could speak freely without fear of being misunderstood.

She was changed in another way, too. Happiness had made her more amiable toward her parents and sisters and brothers. She discovered that, after all, they had more intelligence than she had supposed and more feeling.

And so they were married.

The first year passed very much as their courtship; but when their wedded life had lost its newness, Lyhne could no longer conceal from himself that he wearied of always seeking new expressions for his love. He was tired of donning the plumage of romance and eternally spreading his wings to fly through all the heavens of sentiment and all the abysses of thought. He longed to settle peacefully on his own quiet perch and drowse, with his tired head under the soft, feathery shelter of a wing. He had never conceived of love as an ever-wakeful, restless flame, casting its strong, flickering light into every nook and corner of existence, making everything seem fantastically large and strange. Love to him was more like the quiet glow of embers on their bed of ashes, spreading a gentle warmth, while the faint dusk wraps all distant things in forgetfulness and makes the near seem nearer and more intimate.

He was tired, worn out. He could not stand all this romance. He longed for the firm support of the commonplace under his feet, as a fish, suffocating in hot air, languishes for the clear, fresh coolness of the waves. It must end sometime, when it had run its course. Bartholine was no longer inexperienced either in books or in life. She knew them as well as he. He had given her all he had — and now he was expected to go on giving. It was impossible; he had nothing more. There was only one comfort: Bartholine was with child.

Bartholine had long realized with sorrow that her conception of Lyhne was changing little by little, and that he no longer stood on the dizzy pinnacle to which she had raised him in the days of their courtship. While she did not yet doubt that he was at bottom what she called a poetic nature, she had begun to feel a little uneasy; for the cloven hoof of prose had shown itself once and again. This only made her pursue romance the more ardently, and she tried to bring back the old state of things by lavishing on him a still greater wealth of sentiment and a still greater rapture, but she met so little response that she almost felt as if she were stilted and unnatural. For a while she tried to drag Lyhne with her, in spite of his resistance; she refused to accept what she suspected; but when, at last, the failure of her efforts made her begin to doubt whether her own mind and heart really possessed the treasures she had imagined, then she suddenly left him alone, became cool, silent, and reserved, and often went off by herself to grieve over her lost illusions. For she saw it all now, and was bitterly disappointed to find that Lyhne, in his inmost self, was no whit different from people she used to live among. She had merely been deceived by the very ordinary fact that his love, for a brief moment, had invested him with a fleeting glamour of soulfulness and exaltation — a very common occurrence with persons of a lower nature.

Lyhne was grieved and anxious, too, over the change in their relationship, and tried to mend matters by unlucky attempts at the old
romantic flights, but it all availed nothing except to show Bartholine
yet more clearly how great had been her mistake.

Such was the state of things between man and wife when Bartholine
brought forth her first child. It was a boy, and they called him Niels.

Chapter II

*I*n a way, the child brought the parents together again. Over his little
cradle they would meet in a common hope, a common joy, and a
common fear; of him they would think, and of him they would talk,
each as often and as readily as the other, and each was grateful to the
other for the child and for all the happiness and love he brought.

Yet they were still far apart.

Lyhne was quite absorbed in his farming and the affairs of the parish.
Not that he took the position of a leader or even of a reformer, but he
gave scrupulous attention to the existing order of things, looked on as
an interested spectator, and carried out the cautious improvements
recommended, after deliberate — very deliberate — consideration, by his
old head servant or the elders of the parish.

It never occurred to him to make any use of the knowledge he had
acquired in earlier days. He had too little faith in what he called theories
and far too great respect for the time-hallowed, venerable dogmas of
experience which other people called practical. In fact, there was nothing
about him to indicate that he had not lived here and lived thus all his
life — except one little trait. He had a habit of sitting for half hours at
a time, quite motionless, on a stile or a boundary stone, looking out
over the luscious green rye or the golden top-heavy oats, in a strange,
vegetative trance. This was a relic of other days; it recalled his former
self, the young Lyhne.

Bartholine, in her world, was by no means so ready to adapt herself
quickly and with a good grace. No, she first had to voice her sorrow

through the verses of a hundred poets, lamenting, in all the broad generalities of the period, the thousands of barriers and fetters that oppress humanity. Sometimes her lament would be clothed in lofty indignation, flinging its wordy froth against the thrones of emperors and the dungeons of tyrants; sometimes it would take the form of a calm, pitying sorrow, looking on as the effulgent light of beauty faded from a blind and slavish generation cowed and broken by the soulless bustle of the day; then again it would appear only as a gentle sigh for the freedom of the bird in its flight and of the cloud drifting lightly into the distance.

At last she grew tired of lamenting, and the impotence of her grief goaded her into doubt and bitterness. Like worshipers who beat their saint and tread him under foot when he refuses to show his power, she would scoff at the romance she once idolized, and scornfully ask herself whether she did not expect the bird Roc to appear presently in the cucumber bed, or Aladdin's cave to open under the floor of the milk cellar. She would answer herself in a sort of childish cynicism, pretending that the world was excessively prosaic, calling the moon green cheese and the roses potpourri, all with a sense of taking revenge and at the same time with a half uneasy, half fascinated feeling that she was committing blasphemy.

These attempts at setting herself free were futile. She sank back into the dreams of her girlhood, but with the difference that now they were no longer illumined by hope. Moreover, she had learned that they were only dreams — distant, illusive dreams, which no longing in the world could ever draw down to her earth. When she abandoned herself to them now, it was with a sense of weariness, while an accusing inner voice told her that she was like the drunkard who knows that his passion is destroying him, that every debauch means strength taken from his weakness and added to the power of his desire. But the voice sounded in vain, for a life soberly lived, without the fair vice of dreams, was no life at all — life had exactly the value that dreams gave it and no more.

So widely different, then, were Niels Lyhne's father and mother, the two friendly powers that struggled unconsciously for mastery over his young soul from the moment the first gleam of intelligence in him gave them something to work on. As the child grew older, the struggle became more intense and was waged with a greater variety of weapons.

The faculty in the boy through which the mother tried to influence him was his imagination. He had plenty of imagination, but even when he was a very small boy, it was evident that he felt a great difference between the fairy world his mother's words conjured up and the world that really existed. Often his mother would tell him stories and describe the woeful plight of the hero, until Niels could not see any way out of all this trouble, and could not understand how the misery closing like an impenetrable wall tighter and tighter around him and the hero could be overcome. Then it happened quite a number of times that he would suddenly press his cheek against his mother's and whisper, with eyes full of tears and lips trembling, "But it isn't *really* true?" And when he had received the comforting answer he wanted, he would heave a deep sigh of relief and settle down contentedly to listen to the end.

His mother did not quite like this defection.

When he grew too old for fairy tales, and she tired of inventing them, she would tell him, with some embroideries of her own, about the heroes of war and peace, choosing those that lent themselves to pointing a moral about the power dwelling in a human soul when it wills one thing only and neither allows itself to be discouraged by the short-sighted doubts of the moment nor to be enticed into a soft, enervating peace.

All her stories went to this tune, and when history had no more heroes that suited her, she chose an imaginary hero, one whose deeds and fate she could shape as she pleased — a hero after her own heart, spirit of her spirit, aye, flesh of her flesh and the blood of hers, too.

A few years after Niels was born, she had brought forth a still-born boy child, and him she chose. All that he might have been and done she served up before his brother in a confused medley of Promethean longings, Messianic courage, and Herculean might, with a naïve travesty, a monstrous distortion, a world of cheap fantasies, having no more body of reality than had the tiny little skeleton moldering in the earth of Lonborg graveyard.

Niels was not deceived about the moral of all these tales. He realized perfectly that it was contemptible to be like ordinary people, and he was quite ready to submit to the hard fate that belonged to heroes. In imagination he willingly suffered the wearisome struggles, the ill fortunes, the martyrdom of being misjudged, and the victories without peace; but at the same time he felt a wondrous relief in thinking that it was so far away, that nothing of all this would happen before he was grown up.

As the dream-figures and dream-tones of night may walk abroad in the wakeful day like vapory forms, mere shadows of sound, calling on thought and holding it for a fleeting second, as it listens and wonders whether anyone really called — so the images of that dream-born future whispered softly through Niels Lyhne's childhood, reminding him gently but ceaselessly of the fact that there was a limit set to this happy time, and that presently one day it would be no more.

This consciousness roused in him a craving to enjoy his childhood to the full, to suck it up through every sense, not to spill a drop, not a single one. Therefore his play had intensity, sometimes lashed into a passion, under the pressure of an uneasy sense that time was flowing away from him before he could gather from its treasure-laden waters all they brought, as one wave broke upon another. He would sometimes throw himself down on the ground and sob with despair when a holiday hung heavy on his hands for the lack of one thing or another — playmates, inventiveness, or fair weather — and he hated to go to bed, because sleep was empty of events and devoid of sensation.

Yet it was not always so.

It would sometimes happen that he grew weary, and his imagination ran out of colors. Then he would be quite wretched and feel that he was too small and insignificant for these ambitious dreams. He seemed to himself a mean liar, who had brazenly pretended to love and understand what was great, though if the truth were told, he cared only for the petty, loved only the commonplace, and carried all, all low-born wishes and desires fully alive within himself. Sometimes he would even feel that he had the class hatred of the rabble against everything exalted, and that he would joyfully have helped to stone these heroes who were of a better blood than he and knew that they were.

On such days, he would shun his mother, and, with a sense of following an ignoble instinct, would seek his father, turning a willing ear and receptive mind to the latter's earth-bound thoughts and matter-of-fact explanations. He felt at home with his father and rejoiced in the likeness between them, well-nigh forgetting that it was the same father whom he was wont to look down upon with pity from the pinnacles of his dream castle. Of course this was not present in his childish mind with the clearness and definiteness given it by the spoken word, but it was all there, though unformed, unborn, in a vague and intangible embryo form. It was like the curious vegetation at the bottom of the sea when seen through layers of ice. Break the ice, or draw that which lives in the dimness out into the full light of speech — what happens is the same: that which is now seen and now grasped is not, in its clearness, the shadowy thing that was.

Chapter III

*T*he years passed. One Christmas trod upon the heels of another, leaving the air bright with its festive glow till long after Epiphany. Whitsun after Whitsun scampered over flower-decked meadows. One summer holiday after another drew near, celebrated its orgy of fresh air and sunshine, poured out its fiery wine from brimming goblets, and then vanished, one day, in a sinking sun; only memory lingered with sunburned cheek and wondering eyes and blood that danced.

The years had passed, and the world was no longer the realm of wonder that it had been. The dim recesses behind the moldering elder bushes, the mysterious attic rooms, the gloomy stone passage under the Klastrup road — fancied terrors that once thrilled him no longer lurked there. The hillside that bloomed at the first trill of the lark, hiding the grass under starry, purple-rimmed daisies and yellow buttercups, the fantastic wealth of animals and plants in the river, the wild precipices of the sand-pit, its black rocks and bits of silvery granite — all these were just flowers, animals, and stones; the shining fairy gold had turned into withered leaves again.

One game after another grew old and silly, stupid and tiresome like the pictures in the ABC, and yet they had once been new, inexhaustibly new. Here they used to roll a barrel-hoop — Niels and the pastor's Frithjof — and the hoop was a ship, which was wrecked when it toppled over, but if you caught it before it fell, then it was casting anchor. The narrow passage between the outhouses, where you could hardly squeeze through, was Bab-el-Mandeb or the Portal of Death. On the stable door "England" was written in chalk, and on the barn door "France." The garden gate was Rio de Janeiro, but the smithy was Brazil. Another game was to play Holger the Dane: you *could* play it among the tall burs behind the barn; but if you went up in the miller's pasture, there were two sink-holes known as the gorges, and there were the haunts of the veritable Prince Burmand and his wild Saracens, with reddish grey turbans and yellow plumes in their helmets — burdocks and Aaron's rod of the tallest. That was the only *real* Mauretania. That rank, succulent growth, that teeming mass of exuberant plant life, excited their lust of destruction and intoxicated them with the voluptuous joy of demolishing. The wooden swords gleamed with the brightness of steel; the green sap stained the blade with red gore, and the cut stalks squashing under their feet were Turks' bodies trampled under horses' hoofs with a sound as of bones crunched in flesh.

Sometimes they played down by the fjord; mussel shells were launched as ships, and when the vessel got stuck in a clump of seaweed, or went aground on a sandbank, it was Columbus in the Sargasso Sea or the discovery of America. Harbors and mighty embankments were built; the Nile was dug out in the firm beach sand, and once they made Gurre Castle out of pebbles — a tiny dead fish in an oyster shell was the corpse of Tove, and they were King Valdemar who sat sorrowing by her side.

But this was all past.

Niels was quite a lad now, twelve years old, nearing thirteen, and he no longer needed to hack thistles and burdocks in order to feed his knightly fancies, anymore than he had to launch his explorer's dreams in a mussel shell. A book and a corner of a sofa were enough for him now, and if the book refused to bear him to the coast of his desires, he would hunt up Frithjof and tell him the tales which the book would not yield. Arm in arm, they would saunter down the road, one telling, both listening; but when they wanted to revel to the full and really give their imagination free play, they would hide in the fragrant dimness of the hayloft. After a while, these stories, which always ended just when you had really entered into them, grew into a single long story that never ended, but lived and died with one generation after the other; for when the hero had grown old, or you had been careless enough to let him die, you could always give him a son, who would inherit everything from the father, and whom, in addition, you could dower with any other virtues that you happened to value particularly just at the moment.

Whatever stamped itself on Niels's mind, what he saw, what he understood and what he misunderstood, what he admired and what he knew he ought to admire — all was woven into the story. As running water is colored by every passing picture, sometimes holding the image with perfect clearness, sometimes distorting it or throwing it back in wavering, uncertain lines, then again drowning it completely in the color and play of its own ripples, so the lad's story reflected feeling and thoughts, his own and those of other people, mirrored human beings and events, life and books, as well as it could. It was a play life, running side by side with real life. It was a snug retreat, where you could abandon yourself to dreams of the wildest adventures. It was a fairy garden that opened at your slightest nod, and received you in all its glory, shutting out everybody else. Whispering palms closed overhead; flowers of sunshine and leaves like stars on vines of coral spread at your feet, and among them a thousand paths led to all the ages and the climes. If you followed one, it would lead you to one place, and if you followed another, it would lead you to another place, to Aladdin and Robinson Crusoe, to Vaul-under and Henrik Magnard, to Niels Klim and Mungo Park, to Peter Simple and Odysseus — and the moment you wished it, you were home again.

About a month after Niels's twelfth birthday, two new faces appeared at Lönborggaard.

One was that of the new tutor; the other was that of Edele Lyhne.

The tutor, Mr. Bigum, was a candidate for orders and was at the threshold of the forties. He was rather small, but with a stocky strength like that of a work-horse, broad-chested, high-shouldered, and slightly stooping. He walked with a heavy, slow, deliberate tread, and moved his arms in a vague, expressionless way that seemed to require a great deal of room. His high, wide forehead was flat as a wall, with two perpendicular lines between the eyebrows; the nose was short and blunt, the mouth large with thick, fresh lips. His eyes were his best feature, light in color, mild, and clear. The movements of his eyeballs showed that he was slightly deaf. Nevertheless, he loved music and played his violin with passionate devotion; for the notes, he said, were not heard only with the ears, but with the whole body, eyes, fingers, and feet; if the ear failed sometimes, the hand would find the right note without its aid, by a strange, intuitive genius of its own. Besides, the audible tones were, after all, false, but he who possessed the divine gift of music carried within him an invisible instrument compared to which the most wonderful Cremona was like the stringed calabash of the savage. On this instrument the soul played; its strings gave forth ideal notes, and upon it the great tone poets had composed their immortal works.

The external music, which was borne on the air of reality and heard with the ears, was nothing but a wretched simulation, a stammering attempt to say the unutterable. It resembled the music of the soul as the statue modeled by hands, carved with a chisel, and meted with a measure resembled the wondrous marble dream of the sculptor which no eye ever beheld and no lip ever praised.

Music, however, was by no means Mr. Bigum's chief interest. He was first of all a philosopher, but not one of the productive philosophers who find new laws and build new systems. He laughed at their systems, the snail-shells in which they dragged themselves across the illimitable field of thought, fondly imagining that the field was within the snail-shell! And these laws — laws of thought, laws of nature! Why, the discovery of a law meant nothing but the fixing of your own limitations: I can see so far and no farther — as if there were not another horizon beyond the first, and another and yet another, horizon beyond horizon, law beyond law, in an unending vista! No, he was not that kind of philosopher. He did not think he was vain, or that he overvalued himself, but he could not close his eyes to the fact that his intellect had a wider span than that of other mortals. When he meditated upon the works of the great thinkers, it seemed to him that he strode forward through a region peopled by slumbering thought-giants, who awoke, bathed in the light of his spirit, to consciousness of their own strength. And so it was always; every thought, mood, or sentiment of another person which was vouchsafed the privilege of awakening within him rose up with his sign on its forehead, ennobled, purified, with wings strengthened, endowed with a power and a might that its creator had never dreamed of.

How often had he gazed with an almost humble amazement on the marvelous wealth of his soul and the divine assurance of his spirit! For it would often happen that different days would find him judging the world and the things of the world from entirely divergent points of view, looking at them through hypotheses that were as far apart as night and morning; yet these points of view and hypotheses, which he chose to make his own, never even for one second made him theirs, anymore than the god who had taken on the semblance of a bull or a swan becomes a bull or a swan and ceases to be a god.

And no one suspected what dwelt within him — all passed him by unseeing. But he rejoiced in their blindness and felt his contempt for humanity growing. A day would come when the light of his eye would go out, and the magnificent structure of his mind would crumble to its foundations and become as that which had never been, but no work from his hand, no, not a line, would he leave to tell the tale of what had been lost in him. His genius should not be crowned with thorns by the world's misjudgment, neither should it wear the defiling purple cloak of the world's admiration. He exulted at the thought that generation after generation would be born and die, and the greatest men of all ages would spend years of their life in the attempt to gain what he could have given them if he had chosen to open his hand.

The fact that he lived in such a humble fashion gave him a curious pleasure, simply because there was such a magnificent extravagance in using his mind to teach children, such a wild incongruity in paying for his time with mere daily bread, and such a colossal absurdity in allowing him to earn this bread upon the recommendation of poor, ordinary mortals, who had vouched for him that he knew enough to take upon himself the miserable task of a tutor. And they had given him *non* in his examination for a degree!

Oh, there was rapture in feeling the brutal stupidity of an existence that cast him aside as poor chaff and valued as golden grain the empty husks, while he knew in his own mind that his lightest thoughts was worth a world!

Yet there were other times when the solitude of his greatness weighed upon him and depressed him.

Ah, how often, when he had communed with himself in sacred silence, hour after hour, and then returned again to consciousness of the audible, visible life round about him, had he not felt himself a stranger to its paltriness and corruptibility. Then he had often been like the monk who listened in the monastery woods to a single trill of the paradise bird and, when he came back, found that a century had died. Ah, if the monk was lonely with the generation that lived among the groves he knew, how much more lonely was the man whose contemporaries had not yet been born.

In such desolate moments he would sometimes be seized with a cowardly longing to sink down to the level of the common herd, to share their lowborn happiness, to become a native of their great earth and a citizen of their little heaven. But soon he would be himself again.

The other newcomer was Edele Lyhne, Lyhne's twenty-six-year-old sister. She had lived many years in Copenhagen, first with her mother, who had moved to the city when she became a widow, and, after her mother's death, in the home of a wealthy uncle, Councilor of State Neergaard. The Neergaards entertained on a large scale and went out a great deal, so Edele lived in a whirl of balls and festivities.

She was admired wherever she went, and envy, the faithful shadow of admiration, also followed her. She was talked about as much as one can be without having done anything scandalous, and whenever men discussed the three reigning beauties of the town there were always many voices in favor of striking out one name and substituting that of Edele Lyhne, but they could never agree on which of two others should yield to her — as for the third, it was out of the question.

Yet very young men did not admire her. They were abashed in her presence, and felt twice as stupid as usual when she listened to them with her look of mild toleration — a maliciously emphasized toleration which crushed them with a sense that she had heard it all before and knew it by heart. They made efforts to shine in her eyes and their own by assuming blasé airs, by inventing wild paradoxes, or, when their desperation reached a climax, by making bold declarations; but all these attempts, jostling and crowding one upon the other in the abrupt transitions of youth, were met with the faint shadow of a smile, a deadly smile of boredom, which made the victim redden and feel that he was the one hundred and eleventh fly in the same merciless spider's web.

Moreover, her beauty had neither the softness nor the fire to ensnare young hearts. On older hearts and cooler heads she exercised a peculiar fascination.

She was tall. Her thick, heavy hair was blonde with the faint reddish sheen of ripening wheat, but fairer and curling where it grew in two points low on the nape of her neck. Under the high, clean-cut forehead, her eyebrows were pale and indefinite. The light grey eyes were large and clear, neither accented by the brows nor borrowing fitful shadows from the thin, delicate lids. There was something indeterminate and indeterminable in their expression. They always met you with a full and open gaze, without any of the changeful play of sidelong glances or lightning flashes, but almost unnaturally wakeful, invincible, inscrutable. The vivacity was all in the lower part of the face, the nostrils, the mouth, and the chin. The eyes merely looked on. The mouth was particularly expressive. The lips met in a lovely bow with deep, gracious curves and flexible lines, but their beauty was a little marred by a hardness of the lower lip, which sometimes melted away in a smile, and then again stiffened into something akin to brutality.

The bold sweep of the back and the luxuriant fullness of the bosom, contrasted with the classic severity of the shoulders and arms, gave her an audacity, an exotic fascination, which was enhanced by the gleaming whiteness of her skin and the morbid redness of her lips. The effect was provocative and disquieting.

Her tall, slender figure had a subtle distinction, which she was clever enough to underscore, especially in her ball dresses, with sure and conscious art. In fact, her artistic sense applied to her own person would sometimes speak so loudly from her costume that it barely escaped a hint of bad taste even when most exquisitely tasteful. To many this seemed an added charm.

Nothing could be more punctiliously correct than her behavior. In what she said, and in what she permitted to be said, she kept within the strictest bounds of prudery. Her coquetry consisted in not being coquettish, in being incurably blind to her own power, and never making the slightest distinction between her admirers. For that very reason, they all dreamed intoxicating dreams of the face that must be hidden behind the mask; they believed in a fire under the snow and sensed depravity in her innocence. None of them would have been surprised to hear that she had a secret lover, but neither would they have ventured to guess his name.

This was the way people saw Edele Lyhne.

She had left the city for Lönborggaard, because her health had suffered from the constant round of pleasures, the thousand and one nights of balls and masquerades. Toward the end of the winter, the doctor had declared her lungs to be affected, and had prescribed fresh air, quiet, and milk. All these things she found in abundance in her present abode, but she also found an unceasing boredom, which made her long for Copenhagen before a week had passed. She filled letter after letter with entreaties that she might be allowed to return from her exile, and hinted that homesickness did her more harm than the air did her good. But the doctor had so alarmed her uncle and aunt that they felt it their duty to turn a deaf ear to her lamentations, no matter how pathetic.

It was not so much the social diversions she pined for; it was rather that she craved the sense of feeling her own life mingling with the sound-filled air of the great city, whereas in the country the stillness in thoughts, in words, in eyes — in everything — made her feel as though she heard herself unceasingly and with inescapable distinctness, just as one hears a watch ticking through a sleepless night. And to know that over there they were living exactly as before — it was as if she were lying dead *in* the quiet night and heard the strains of music from a ballroom stealing on the air over her grave.

There was no one she could talk to. No one of them all ever caught just the shade of meaning that was the essence of what she said. Of course, they understood her after a fashion, inasmuch as she spoke Danish, but it was a dull, general sort of a way, just as they might have understood a foreign language which they heard only once in a while. They never had the slightest idea of whom or what was meant by a particular intonation of a word, never dreamed that such a little phrase was a quotation, or that another, used in just such a way, was a new variation of a popular witticism. As for their own speech, it had a decent leanness through which one could positively feel the grammatical ribs, and the words were used with a literalness as if they had just come fresh from the columns of the dictionary. Even the way they said Copenhagen! Sometimes with a mysterious emphasis, as if it were a place where people ate little children; then again with a faraway expression, as if they were speaking of a town in central Africa, or in a festive voice tremulous with history, as they might have said Nineveh or Carthage. The pastor always said Axelstead with a reminiscent rapture, as if it had been the name of one of his old sweethearts. Not one of them could say Copenhagen so that it meant the city stretching from Vesterport to the Custom House on both sides of Östergade and Kongens Nytorv. And so it was with all they said and all they did.

There was not a thing at Lönborggaard that did not displease her; these mealtimes regulated by the sun, this smell of lavender in chests and presses, these Spartan chairs, all these provincial pieces of furniture that stood shrinking against the walls as if they were afraid of people! Even the very air was distasteful to her; she could never take a walk without bringing home a robust perfume of meadow-hay and wild flowers, as if she had been locked up in a haymarket.

And then to be called aunt, Aunt Edele. How it grated on her ears! She got used to it after a while, but in the beginning it made the relation between her and Niels rather cool.

Niels didn't care.

Then came a Sunday in the early part of August, when Lyhne and his wife had gone out in the carriage to pay a visit, and Niels and Miss Edele were home alone. In the morning Edele had asked Niels to pick some cornflowers for her, but he had forgotten it. Suddenly, in the afternoon, as he was walking with Frithjof, he remembered, gathered a bouquet, and ran up to the house with it.

Everything was so still that he imagined his aunt must be asleep, and crept silently through the house. At the threshold of the sitting room he stopped, with bated breath, preparing to approach Edele's door. The sitting room was flooded with sunshine, and a blossoming oleander made the air heavy with its sweet fragrance. There was no sound except a muffled splash from the flower stand whenever the goldfish moved in their glass bowls.

Niels crossed the room, balancing himself with outstretched arms, his tongue between his teeth. Cautiously he grasped the doorknob, which was so hot with the sun that it burned his hand, and turned it slowly and carefully, knitting his brows and half closing his eyes. He pulled the door toward him, bent in through the narrow opening, and laid the flowers on a chair just within. The room was dark as if the shades were down, and the air seemed moist with fragrance, the fragrance of attar of roses. As he stooped, he saw only the light straw matting on the floor, the wainscoting under the window, and the lacquered foot of a Gueridon; but when he straightened himself to back out of the door he caught sight of his aunt.

She was stretched full-length on a couch of sea-green satin, dressed in a fanciful gypsy costume. As she lay on her back, chin up, throat tense, and forehead low, her loosened hair flowed down over the end of the couch and along the rug. An artificial pomegranate flower looked as if it had been washed ashore on an island made by a little bronze-colored shoe in the midst of the dull golden stream.

The motley colors of her dress were rich and mellow. Dull blue, pale rose, grey, and orange were blended in the pattern of a little low-cut bodice of a thick, lusterless stuff. Underneath, she wore a white silk chemise with wide sleeves falling to the elbow. The white had a faint pinkish tone, and was shot with threads of reddish gold. Her skirt of pansy-colored velvet without any border was gathered loosely around her, and slid down over the side of the couch in slanting folds. Her feet and legs were bare, and around her crossed ankles she had wound a necklace of pale corals. An open fan was lying on the floor, showing its pattern of playing cards arranged in a wheel, and a little farther away a pair of leaf-brown silk stockings had been thrown, one partly rolled up, the other spread out and revealing the red clock.

At the same moment that Niels caught sight of her, she saw him. Involuntarily she made a slight movement as if to rise, but checked herself and lay still as before, only turning her head a little to look at the boy with a questioning smile.

"I brought these," he said, and went over to her with the flowers.

She held out her hand, glanced at them and then at her costume, comparing the colors, and dropped them with a wearily murmured "Impossible!"

Niels would have picked them up, but she stopped him with a motion of her hand.

"Give me that!" she said, pointing to a red flask that lay on a crumpled handkerchief at her feet.

Niels went to take it. His face was crimson, as he bent over the milk-white, gently rounded legs and the long, slender feet, which had almost the intelligence of a hand in their fine flexible curves. He felt dizzy, and when one foot suddenly turned and bent downward with a quick movement, he almost fell.

"Where did you pick the flowers?" Edele asked.

Niels pulled himself together and turned toward her: "I picked them in the pastor's rye field," he said, in a voice that sounded strange to himself. He handed her the flask without looking up.

Edele noticed his emotion and looked at him astonished. Suddenly she blushed, raised herself on one arm, and drew her feet under her petticoat. "Go, go, go, go!" she said, half peevishly, half shyly, and at every word she sprayed him with the attar of roses.

Niels went. When he was out of the room, she let her feet glide slowly down from the couch and looked at them curiously.

Running with unsteady steps, he hurried through the house to his own room. He felt quite stunned; there was a strange weakness in his knees and a choking sensation in his throat. He threw himself down on the couch and closed his eyes, but it was of no avail, a strange restlessness possessed him; his breath came heavily as in fear, and the light tortured him in spite of his closed eyelids.

Little by little a change came over him. A hot, heavy breath seemed to blow on him and make him helplessly weak. He felt as one in a dream who hears someone calling and tries to go, but cannot move a foot, and is tortured by his weakness, sickens with his longing to get away, is lashed to madness by this calling which does not know one is bound. And he sighed impatiently as if he were ill and looked around quite lost. Never had he felt so miserable, so lonely, so forsaken, and so forlorn.

He sat down in the flood of sunlight from the window, and wept.

From that day Niels felt a timid happiness in Edele's presence. She was no more a human being like anyone else, but an exalted creature, divine by virtue of her strange, mystic beauty. His heart throbbed with rapture in merely looking at her, kneeling to her in his heart, crawling to her feet in abject self-effacement. Yet there were moments when his adoration had to have vent in outward signs of subjection. At such times he would lie in wait for a chance to steal into Edele's room and go through a fixed rite of a certain interminable number of kisses lavished on the little rug in front of her bed, her shoe, or any other object that presented itself to his idolatry.

He regarded it as a piece of great good fortune that his Sunday jacket happened to be degraded, just then, to everyday use; for the lingering scent of attar of roses was like a mighty talisman with which he could conjure up in a magic mirror the image of Edele as he had seen her lying on the green couch wearing her masquerade costume. In the story he and Frithjof were telling each other, this image was ever present, and from now on the wretched Frithjof was never safe from barefooted princesses. If he dragged himself through the dense primeval forest, they would call to him from hammocks of vines. If he sought shelter from the storm in a mountain cave, they would rise from their couches of velvety moss to welcome him, and when he dashed, bloody and smoke-blackened, into the pirate's cabin, shivering the door with a tremendous blow of his saber, he found them there too, resting on the captain's green sofa. They bored him terribly, and he could not see why they should suddenly have become so necessary to their beloved heroes.

*N*o matter in how exalted a place a human being may set his throne, no matter how firmly he may press the tiara of the exceptional, that is genius, upon his brow, he can never be sure that he may not, like Nebuchadnezzar, be seized with a sudden desire to go on all-fours and eat grass and herd with the common beasts of the field.

That was what happened to Mr. Bigum when he quite simply fell in love with Miss Edele, and it availed him nothing that he distorted history to find an excuse for his love by calling Edele Beatrice or Laura or Vittoria Colonna, for all the artificial halos with which he tried to crown his love were blown out as fast as he could light them by the stubborn fact that it was Edele's beauty he was in love with; nor was it the graces of her mind and heart that had captivated him, but her elegance, her air of fashion, her easy assurance, even her graceful insolence. It was a kind of love that might well fill him with shamed surprise at the inconsistency of the children of men.

And what did it all matter! Those eternal truths and makeshift lies that were woven ring in ring to form the heavy armor he called his principles, what were they against his love? If they really were the strength and marrow and kernel of life, then let them show their strength; if they were weaker, let them break; if stronger —. But they were already broken, plucked to pieces like the mesh of rotten threads they were. What did she care about eternal truths? And the mighty visions, how did they help him? Thoughts that plumbed the unfathomable, could they win her? All that he possessed was worthless. Even though his soul shone with the radiance of a hundred suns, what did it avail, when his light was hidden under the ugly fustian of a Diogenes' mantle? Oh, for beauty! Take my soul and give me my thirty pieces of silver — Alcibiades' body, Don Juan's mantle, and a court chamberlain's rank!

But, alas, he had none of these graces, and Edele was by no means attracted to his heavy, philosophic nature. His habit of seeing life in barbarously naked abstractions gave him a noisy dogmaticism, an unpleasant positiveness that jarred her like a misplaced drum in a concert of soft music. The strained quality of his mind, which always seemed to knit its muscles and strike an attitude before every little question like a strong man about to play with iron balls, seemed to her ridiculous. He irritated her by his censorious morality, which pounced on every lightly sketched feeling, indiscreetly tearing away its incognito, rudely calling it by name, just as it was about to flit past him in the course of conversation.

Bigum knew very well what an unfavorable impression he made and how hopeless his love was, but he knew it as we know a thing when we hope with all the strength of our soul that our knowledge is false. There is always the miracle left; and though miracles do not happen, they might happen. Who knows? Perhaps our intelligence, our instinct, our senses, in spite of their daylight clearness, are leading us astray. Perhaps the one thing needful is just that unreasoning courage which follows hope's will-o'-the-wisp as it burns over seething passions pregnant with desire! It is only when we have heard the door of destiny slam shut that we begin to feel the iron-cold talons of certainty digging into our breast, gathering slowly, slowly around our heart, and fastening their clutches upon the fine thread of hope on which our world of happiness hangs: then the thread is severed; then all that it held falls and is shattered; then the shriek of despair sounds through the emptiness.

In doubt, no one despairs.

On a sunny afternoon in September, Edele was sitting on the landing of the half-dozen broad, old-fashioned steps that led down from the summer parlor into the garden. Behind her, the French windows were wide open, flung back against the motley wall-covering of bright red and green vines. She leaned her head against a chair piled high with large black portfolios, and held an etching up before her with both hands. Color prints of Byzantine mosaics in blue and gold were scattered on the pale green rush matting that covered the boards of the landing, on the threshold, and on the oak-brown parquet floor of the summer parlor. At the foot of the steps lay a white shade hat; for Edele's hair was uncovered, with no ornament but a flower of gold filigree in a pattern to match the gold bracelet she wore high on her arm. Her white dress was of semi-transparent stuff with narrow silky stripes; it had an edging of twisted orange and black chenille and tiny rosettes in the same two colors. Light silk mitts covered her hands and reached to the elbow. They were pearl grey like her shoes.

The yellow sunlight was filtered through the drooping branches of an ancient ash. It pierced the cool dimness, forming distinct lines of light, powdering the air with gold dust, and painting the steps, the wall, and the doors with spots of light, spot of sun upon spot of sun, like a perforated shade. Through the tracery of shadow, each color rose to meet the light: white from Edele's dress, blood-red from crimson lips, amber from yellow-blonde hair, and a hundred other tints round about, blue and gold, oak-brown, glitter of glass, red and green.

Edele dropped the etching and looked up despondently, her eyes expressing the silent plaint she was too weary to give vent to in a sigh. Then she settled down as if to shut out her surroundings and withdraw within herself.

Just then Mr. Bigum appeared.

Edele looked at him with a drowsy blinking like that of a child who is too sleepy and comfortable to stir, but too curious to shut its eyes.

Mr. Bigum wore his new beaver hat. He was absorbed in his own thoughts, and gesticulated with his tombac watch in his hand, until the thin silver chain threatened to snap. With a sudden, almost vicious movement, he thrust the watch deep down into his pocket, threw back his head impatiently, caught the lapel of his coat in a peevish grasp, and would have gone on with an angry jerk of his whole body, his face darkened by all the hopeless rage that boils in a man when he is running away from his own torturing thoughts, and knows that he runs in vain.

Edele's hat, lying at the foot of the steps and shining white against the black earth of the walk, stopped him in his flight. He picked it up with both hands, then caught sight of Edele, and as he stood trying to think of something to say, he held it instead of giving it to her. Not an idea could he find in his brain; not a word would be born on his tongue, and he looked straight ahead with a stupid expression of arrested profundity.

"It is a hat, Mr. Bigum," said Edele carelessly, to break the embarrassed silence.

"Yes," said the tutor eagerly, delighted to hear her confirm a likeness that had struck him also; but the next moment he blushed at his clumsy answer.

"It was lying here," he added hurriedly, "here on the ground like this — just like this," and he bent down to show where it had lain with an inconsequential minuteness born of his confusion. He felt almost happy in his relief at having given some sign of life, however futile. He was still standing with the hat in his hand.

"Do you intend to keep it?" asked Edele.

Bigum had no answer to that.

"I mean will you give it to me?" she explained.

Bigum came a few steps nearer and handed her the hat. "Miss Lyhne," she said, "you think — you must not think — I beg you to let me speak; that is — I am not saying anything, but be patient with me! — I love you, Miss Lyhne, unutterably, unutterably, beyond all words I love you. Oh, if language held a word that combined the cringing admiration of the slave, the ecstatic smile of the martyr, and the gnawing homesickness of the exile, with that word I could tell you my love. Oh, listen to me, do not thrust me away yet! Do not think that I am insulting you with an insane hope! I know how insignificant I seem in your eyes, how clumsy and repulsive, yes, repulsive. I am not forgetting that I am poor, — you must know it, — so poor that I have to let my mother live in a charitable institution, and I can't help it, can't help it. I am so miserably poor. Yes, Miss Lyhne, I am only a poor servant in your brother's house, and yet there is a world where I am ruler, powerful, proud, rich, with the crown of victory, noble by virtue of the passion that drove Prometheus to steal the fire from the heaven of the gods. There I am brother to all the great in spirit, whom the earth has borne, and who bear the earth. I understand them as none but equals understand one another; no flight that they have flown is too high for the strength of my wings. Do you understand me? Do you believe me? Oh, don't believe me! It isn't true, I am nothing but the Kobold figure you see before you. It is all past; for this terrible madness of love has paralyzed my wings, the eyes of my spirit have lost their sight, my heart is dried up, my soul is drained to bloodless poltroonery. Oh, save me from myself, Miss Lyhne, don't turn away in scorn! Weep over me, weep, it is Rome burning!"

He had fallen to his knees on the steps, wringing his hands. His face was blanched and distorted, his teeth were clinched in agony, his eyes drowned in tears; his whole body shook under the suppressed sobs that were heard only as a gasping for breath.

"Control yourself, Mr. Bigum," she said in a slightly too compassionate tone. "Control yourself, don't give way so, be a man! Please get up and go down into the garden a little while and try to pull yourself together."

"And you can't love me at all!" groaned Mr. Bigum almost inaudibly. "Oh, it's terrible! There is not a thing in my soul that I wouldn't murder and degrade if I could win you thereby. No, no, even if anyone offered me madness and I could possess you in my hallucinations, *possess* you, then I would say: Take my brain, tear down its wonderful structure with rude hands, break all the fine threads that bind my spirit to the resplendent triumphal chariot of the human mind, and let me sink in the mire of the physical, under the wheels of the chariot, and let others follow the shining paths that lead to the light! Do you understand me? Can you comprehend that even if your love came to me robbed of its glory, debased, befouled, as a caricature of love, as a diseased phantom, I would receive it kneeling as if it were the Sacred Host? But the best in me is useless, the worst in me is useless, too. I cry to the sun, but it does not shine; to the statue, but it does not answer — answer. . . ! What is there to answer except that I suffer? No, these unutterable torments that rend my whole being down to its deepest roots, this anguish is nothing to you but an impertinence. You feel nothing but a little cold offence; in your heart you laugh scornfully at the poor tutor and his impossible passion."

"You do me an injustice, Mr. Bigum," said Edele, rising, while Mr. Bigum rose too. "I am not laughing. You ask me if there is no hope, and I answer: No, there is no hope. That is surely nothing to laugh at. But there is one thing I want to say to you. From the first moment you began to think of me, you must have known what my answer would be, and you did know it, did you not? You knew it all the time, and yet you have been lashing all your thoughts and desires on toward the goal which you knew you could not reach. I am not offended by your love, Mr. Bigum, but I condemn it. You have done what so many people do: they close their eyes to the realities and stop their ears when life cries 'No' to their wishes. They want to forget the deep chasm fate has placed between them and the object of their ardent longing. They want their dream to be fulfilled. But life takes no account of dreams. There isn't a single obstacle that can be dreamed out of the world, and in the end we lie there crying at the edge of the chasm, which hasn't changed and is just where it always was. But we have changed, for we have let our dreams goad all our thoughts and spur all our longings to the very highest tension. The chasm is no narrower, and everything in us cries out with longing to reach the other side, but no, always no, never anything else. If we had only kept a watch on ourselves in time! But now it is too late, now we are unhappy."

She paused almost as if she woke from a trance. Her voice had been quiet, groping, as if she were speaking to herself, but now it hardened into a cold aloofness.

"I cannot help you, Mr. Bigum. You are nothing to me of what you wish to be. If that makes you unhappy, you must be unhappy; if you suffer, you must suffer-there are always some who have to suffer. If you make a human being your god and the ruler of your fate, you must bow to the will of divinity, but it is never wise to make yourself gods, or to give your soul over to another; for there are gods who will not step down from their pedestals. Be sensible, Mr. Bigum! Your god is so small and so little worth your worship; turn from it and be happy with one of the daughters of the land."

With a faint little smile, she went in through the summer parlor, while Mr. Bigum looked after her, crestfallen. For another fifteen minutes he walked up and down before the steps. All the words that had been spoken seemed to be still vibrating through the air; she had so lately gone, it seemed that her shadow must still linger there; it seemed that she could not yet be out of reach of his prayers, and everything could not be inexorably ended. But after a while the chambermaid came out and gathered up the engravings, carried in the chair, the portfolios, the rush matting — everything.

Then he could go too.

In the open gable window up above, Niels sat gazing after him. He had heard the whole conversation from beginning to end. His face had a frightened look and a nervous trembling passed through his body. For the first time he was afraid of life. For the first time his mind grasped the fact that when life has sentenced you to suffer, the sentence is neither a fancy nor a threat, but you *are* dragged to the rack, and you *are* tortured, and there is no marvelous rescue at the last moment, no awakening as from a bad dream.

He felt it as a foreboding which struck him with terror.

*E*dele did not have a good autumn, and the winter drained her strength completely. Spring, when it came, did not find one poor little life-germ that it could warm and coax into growth; it found only a withering, which no gentleness and no warmth could arrest or even retard. But it could at least pour a flood of light over the paling life and caress the ebbing strength with fragrant, balmy air, as the evening crimson follows slowly in the wake of dying day.

The end came in May, on a day flooded with sunshine, one of the days when the lark is never silent, and you can almost see the rye grow. The great cherry trees outside her window were white with flowers — nosegays of snow, wreaths of snow, cupolas, arches, garlands, a fairy architecture against the bluest of skies.

She was very weak that day, and withal she felt a strange sense of lightness. She knew what was coming, for that morning she had sent for Bigum and said good-bye to him.

Her uncle had come over from Copenhagen, and all that afternoon the handsome, white-haired man sat by her bedside with his hand folded in her hands. He did not speak, but once in a while he would move his hand, and she would press it; she would look up, and he would smile to her. Her brother, too, was in the room, gave her medicine, and helped her in other ways.

She lay very still with closed eyes, while familiar pictures from life over there flitted past her. Sorgenfri with hanging birches, the red church at Lyngby standing on a foundation of graves, and the white country house with the bit of sunken road leading down to the sea, where the paling always was green as if painted by the water — the images took shape before her, grew clear, melted away, and vanished. And other pictures came. There was Bredgade when the sun went down, and the darkness closed in around the houses. There was the queer Copenhagen you found when you came in from the country in the forenoon. It seemed so weird with its hurry and bustle in the sunlight, with the whitened windowpanes and the streets smelling of fruit. There was something unreal about the houses in the strong light; the noise and rattle of wheels could not chase away the silence that seemed to enfold them. . . . Then came the dim, quiet drawing room in the autumn evenings, when she was dressed for the theater, and the others were not down yet — the smell of incense, the wood fire from the stove lighting up the carpet — the rain whipping the windows — the horses stamping at the door — the melancholy cry of the mussel venders . . . and back of all this the theater awaiting her with light and music and festive glow.

With such pictures the afternoon wore away.

Niels and his mother were in the parlor. Niels knelt by the sofa with his face pressed down against its brown velvet and his hands clasped over his head. He wept and wailed aloud, giving himself up to his grief without any attempt at self-control. Mrs. Lyhne sat beside him. The hymn book lay on the table in front of her, open at the hymns usually sung at funerals. Now and then she read a few verses, and sometimes she would bend down over her son to speak a word of soothing or chiding, but Niels would not be comforted, and she could not stop his weeping or the wild prayers born of his despair.

Presently Lyhne appeared in the door of the sick-room. He made no signs, but looked at them so solemnly that both rose and followed him in to his sister. He took them by the hand and led them to the bed. Edele looked up and gazed at each one in turn, while her lips motioned for words. Then Lyhne took his wife over to the window and sat down there with her. Niels threw himself on his knees at the foot of the bed.

He wept softly and prayed with clasped hands, eagerly and incessantly, in a low, passionate whisper. He told God that he would not stop hoping. "I won't let You go, Lord, I won't let You go before You have said 'Yes'! You mustn't take her away from us; for You know how we love her — You mustn't, You mustn't, Oh! I can't say. 'Thy will be done;' for Your will is to let her die, but, oh, let her live! I will thank You and obey You. I will do everything I know You want me to do. I'll be so good and never offend You, if You will only let her live! Do You hear, God? Oh, stop, stop, and make her well before it's too late! I will, I will, oh, what can I promise You? — Oh, I'll thank You, never, never, forget You; oh, but hear me! Don't You see she's dying, don't You see she's dying? Do You hear? Take Your hand away! I can't lose her, God, I can't! Let her live, won't You please, won't You please? Oh, it's wicked of You —"

Outside, beyond the window, the white flowers flushed to pink in the light of the setting sun. Arch upon arch, the blossoming sprays built of their gossamer bloom a rose castle, a vaulted choir of roses, and through this airy dome the azure sky shone with a softened twilight blue, while golden lights and lights of gold flaming to crimson shot like the rays of a nimbus from every garlanded line of the ethereal temple.

White and still, Edele lay there with the old man's hand between both of hers. Slowly she breathed out her life, breath by breath; fainter and fainter was the rising of her breast; heavier and heavier fell the eyelids.

"My love to Copenhagen!" was her last low whisper.

But her last message was heard by no one. It did not come from her lips even as a breath — her message to him, the great artist whom she had loved secretly with her whole soul, but to whom she had been nothing, only a name that his ear knew, only one unrecognized figure in the great admiring public.

The light faded into blue dusk, and her hands fell weakly apart. The shadows grew — shadows of night and of death.

The old man bent down over her head and laid his hands on her pulse, waiting quietly, and when the last throb of life had ebbed away, when the last feeble pulse beat was stilled, he lifted the pale hand to his lips.

"Little Edele!"

Chapter IV

*T*here are those who can take up their grief and bear it, strong natures who feel their own powers through the very heaviness of their burden. Weaker people give themselves up to their sorrow passively, as they would submit to a sickness; and like a sickness their sorrow pervades them, drinks itself into their innermost being and becomes a part of them, is assimilated in them through a slow struggle, and finally loses itself in them, as they return to perfect health.

But there are yet others to whom sorrow is a violence done them, a cruelty which they never learn to accept as a trial or chastisement or as simple fate. It is to them an act of tyranny, an expression of personal hate, and it always leaves a sting in their hearts.

Children do not often grieve in this way, but Niels Lyhne did. For had he not been face to face with God in the fervor of his prayers? Had he not crawled on his knees to the foot of the throne, full of hope, tremulous with fear, and yet firm in his faith in the omnipotence of prayer, with courage to plead until he should be heard? And he had been forced to rise from the dust and go away with his hope put to shame. His faith had not been able to bring the miracle down from heaven, no God had answered his cry, death had marched straight on and seized its prey, as if no sheltering wall of prayers had been lifted toward the sky.

A stillness fell upon him. His faith had flung itself blindly against the gates of heaven, and now it lay on Edele's grave with broken wings. For he had believed with the crude, implicit fairy-tale faith that children so often feel. The complex, subtly shaded figure of the Catechism is not the God children believe in; their God is the mighty one in the Old Testament, He who loved Adam and Eve so much, and to whom the whole generation of men, kings, prophets, Pharaohs, are nothing but good and bad children, this tremendous, fatherly God, who is wrathful with the anger of a giant and bountiful with the generosity of a giant, Who has hardly created life before He lets death loose upon it, Who drowns His earth in the waters from His heaven, who thunders down laws too heavy for the race He made, and who, finally, in the days of the Emperor Augustus, has pity upon men and sends His Son to death in order that the law may be broken while it is fulfilled. This God, Who always answers with a miracle, is the one to whom children speak when they pray. By and by, a day comes when they understand that they have heard His voice for the last time in the earthquake that shook Golgotha and opened the graves, and that now, since the veil of His Holy of Holies has been rent in twain, it is the God Jesus who reigns; and from that day on they pray differently.

But Niels had not yet attained to this. It is true, he had followed Jesus on His earthly pilgrimage with a believing heart, but when he saw Him subjecting Himself to the Father, going about so bereft of power and suffering so humanly, all this had hidden the godhead from him. He had seen in Him only the one Who did the will of the Father, the Son of God, not God Himself: therefore, it was to God the Father he had prayed, and it was God the Father who had failed him in his bitter need. But if God had turned from him, he could turn from God. If God had no ears, he had no lips; if God had no compassion, he had no worship, and he defied and cast God out of his heart.

On the day Edele was buried, he spumed the earth of the grave with his foot, whenever the pastor spoke the name of the Lord, and when he met it afterwards in books or on the lips of people, a rebellious frown would wrinkle his youthful forehead. When he lay down to sleep at night, a sense of forsaken greatness came over him, as he thought that now all the others, children and grown people, were praying to the Lord and closing their eyes in His name, while he alone held his hands from clasping in prayer, he alone refused to do God homage. He was shut out from the sheltering care of Heaven. No angel watched by his side; alone and unprotected, he drifted on the strangely murmuring waters of darkness, and loneliness enfolded him, spreading out from his bed in ever widening and receding circles. Still he did not pray; though he longed till tears came, he did not call.

And it was so all his life. He had freed himself defiantly from the point of view imposed upon him by his teachers, and he fled with his sympathy to the side of those who had wasted their strength in vainly kicking against the pricks. In the books he had been given to read and in what he had been taught, God and His chosen people and ideas marched on in an endless triumphal procession, and he had joined in the jubilant shouting, had exulted in the sense of being counted with the proud legions of the conqueror; for is not victory always righteous, and is not the victor a liberator, a reformer, a light bringer?

But now the shouting had died down. Now he was silent, and he began to enter into the thoughts of the defeated and feel with the hearts of the vanquished. He understood that even when that which prevails is good, that which yields is not therefore bad. He went over to the losing side and told himself that this was finer and greater. The power of the victor he called mere brute force and violence. He took sides — as whole-heartedly as he could — against God, but as a vassal who takes up arms against his liege lord; for he still believed, and could not drive out his faith by defiance.

His tutor, Mr. Bigum, was not one who could lead a soul back to the old paths. Indeed, his temperamental philosophy, by virtue of which he could be fired and enraptured by each and every side of the question-today one; tomorrow, another — set all dogmas adrift in the minds of his pupils. At bottom he was really a man of Christian principles, and if anyone could have pinned him down saying what was the fixed point in all this fluid matter, he would most likely have replied that it was the creed of the Evangelical Lutheran Church or something akin to that, but he himself had very little inclination to drive his pupils along the straight road of orthodoxy or to warn them at every step that the least deviation from the beaten track meant straying into lies and darkness, likely to end in perdition and hell; for he had none of the passionate concern of the orthodox for jots and tittles. He was, in fact, religious in the slightly artistic, superior manner such talented people affect, not afraid of a little harmonizing, easily enticed into half unconscious rearrangements and adaptations, because, whatever they do, they must assert their own personality, and, in whatever spheres they fly, must hear the whirring of their own wings.

Such people do not guide, but their instruction has a fullness, a copiousness, and a wobbly many-sidedness which, provided they do not utterly confuse a pupil, tend to develop his independence in a high degree, since they almost force him to make up his mind for himself. For children can never rest upon anything vague or indefinite; their very instinct of self-preservation demands a plain Yes or a plain No, a for or against, to show them where to turn with their hate and where with their love.

Hence there was no firm and immutable authority that might have guided Niels with its constant clinching of arguments and pointing of ways. He had taken the bit in his teeth, and plunged headlong on any path that opened before him, provided only that it led him away from what had been the home of his feelings and of his thoughts.

He felt a new sense of power in thus seeing with his own eyes and choosing with his own heart and forming himself by his own will. Many new things came to his mind; traits of his own nature that he had never thought of and that seemed unrelated one to the other, fitted themselves together wonderfully and were fused into a rational whole. It was a fascinating time of discovery. Little by little, in fear and uncertain exultation, in incredulous joy, he found himself. He began to realize that he was not like others, and a new spiritual modesty made him shy, awkward, and taciturn. He grew suspicious of questions, and imagined he found hints of his own most hidden thoughts in everything that was said. Having learned to read in his own heart, he supposed everybody else could read what was written there, and he shunned his elders, preferring to roam about alone. It seemed to him that people had suddenly become very intrusive; he developed a slightly hostile feeling toward them as to creatures of another race, and in his loneliness he began to hold them up for scrutiny and judgment. Formerly the names of father, mother, the pastor, the miller, sufficed to characterize, and the name had quite hidden the person from him. But now he saw that the pastor was a jolly little man, who made himself as meek and demure as he could at home to escape the notice of his wife, while abroad he tried to forget the domestic yoke by talking himself into a frenzy of rebellion and loud-voiced thirst for liberty. That was the pastor as he saw him now.

And Mr. Bigum?

He had seen him ready to throw everything overboard for Edele's love, had heard him deny himself and the soul within him in that hour of passion in the garden, and now he was always talking about the philosopher rising in Olympic calm above the vague whirlwinds and mist-born rainbows of life. It roused a painful contempt in the lad and made his doubts sleep but lightly, ready to wake in a moment. For how could he know that the very things in human nature which Mr. Bigum called by belittling names were otherwise christened when they appeared in himself, and that his Olympic calm toward that which moves common mortals was but a Titan's disdainful smile, quick with memories of a Titan's longing and a Titan's passions.

Chapter V

Six months had passed since Edele's death, when one of Lyhne's cousins, Mrs. Refstrup, became a widow. Her husband had been a potter, but the business had never been flourishing, and during his long illness it had quite run to seed, so there was scarcely anything between the widow and actual want. Seven children were more than she could provide for. The two youngest and also the oldest, who could help her in the factory, remained with her, but the others were distributed among the family. The Lyhnes took the second boy, Erik, who was fourteen, and had been studying at the Latin school in the nearest town, where he had free tuition. Now he was to share Mr. Bigum's instruction with Niels and Frithjof Petersen, the pastor's boy.

It was very much against his will that he was kept at his books, for he wanted to be a sculptor. His father had called this nonsense, but Lyhne had nothing against it; he said the boy had talent. Still he thought he ought to take his bachelor's degree first, in order to have something to fall back upon; and besides a classical education was necessary to a sculptor, or was, at least, very desirable. That settled the matter for the time being. Erik had to console himself with the fairly large collection of good engravings and neat bronzes that Lönborggaard had to offer. This meant a great deal to one who had seen nothing but the rubbish bequeathed the local library by a bone-carver more freakish than artistic in taste, and Erik was soon busy with pencil and modeling stick. No one attracted him as did Guido Reni, who in those days was more famous than Raphael and the greatest; nor is there anything that can open young eyes to the beauty of a work of art better than the certainty that their admiration is authorized up to the highest pinnacle. Andrea del Sarto, Parmigianino, and Luini, who were to mean so much to him later when he and his talent had found each other, left him quite indifferent, while the boldness of Tintoretto and the bitterness of Salvator Rosa and Caravaggio filled him with delight. For sweetness in

art has no appeal for the very young; the daintiest of miniature painters
begins his career in the footsteps of Buonarotti, and the pleasantest of
lyrists sets out on his first voyage under the black sail of bloody tragedy.

Still Erik's art was to him only a game, only a little better than other
games, and he was no more proud of a well-modeled head or a cleverly
carved horse than of hitting the weather vane on the church steeple with
a stone, or of swimming out to Sonderhagen and back again without
resting. These were the games in which he excelled, games requiring
physical prowess, strength, endurance, a sure hand, and a practiced eye.
He cared nothing for the kind of sport Niels and Frithjof liked, where
fancy plays the leading role, and all the events and triumphs are
imagined. The result was that the other two soon left their old pastime
to follow Erik's lead. Their romance books were laid aside, and the
interminable story came to a rather violent end one day at a secret
session in the hayloft. Silence brooded over its newly filled grave. In
fact, they shrank from mentioning it to Erik, for he had not been with
them many days before they suspected that he would make fun of them
and their story, that he would shame them and lower them in their own
eyes. He had the power to do this because he himself was so free from
all daydreams and fancies and enthusiasms. His clear, boyish common
sense was as merciless in its perfect healthfulness and as contemptuous
of mental idiosyncrasies as children generally are of physical blemishes.
For that reason Niels and Frithjof were afraid of him. They formed
themselves after him, denied much and concealed more. Niels was
especially quick to suppress in himself anything that was not of Erik's
world, and with the burning zeal of the renegade, he scoffed at Frithjof,
whose slower, more faithful nature could not instantly throw over the
old for the new. His unkind mockery really sprang from jealousy, for
he had fallen in love with Erik on the very first day, while the latter, in
shy aloofness, half reluctant, half supercilious, just barely and grudgingly allowed himself to be loved.

Among all the emotional relations of life is there any that is finer,
more sensitive, and more fervent than the exquisitely modest love of
one boy for another boy? It is a love that never speaks and never dares
to vent itself in a caress or a look, a seeing love that grieves bitterly over
every fault in the loved one, a love made up of longing and admiration
and self-forgetfulness, of pride and humility and calmly breathing
happiness.

Erik stayed at Lönborggaard only a little over a year. It happened that
Lyhne, on a visit to Copenhagen, took occasion to speak about the boy
to one of the leading sculptors there, and showed him some of Erik's
sketches, whereupon Mikkelsen, the sculptor, declared that this was
talent, and further studying was a waste of time. It did not require much

classical education to find a Greek name for a nude figure. So it was settled that Erik was to be sent at once to the city to attend the Academy and work in Mikkelsen's studio.

On the last afternoon, Niels and Erik were sitting in their room, Niels looking at the pictures in a penny magazine, Erik deep in Spengler's critical catalogue of the art collection at Christiansborg. How often he had turned the leaves of this book and tried to form a conception of the pictures from its naïve description! Sometimes he would get almost sick with longing to behold all this art and beauty with his own eyes, to grasp it in very truth and make that glory of line and color his own by the mere strength of his enthusiasm. And how often, too, he had closed the book, weary of gazing into that drifting, fantastic mist of words which refused to solidify and take shape, refused to give forth anything, but went on in a vague and confused shifting — flowing and slipping away — flowing and slipping away.

But today it was all different. Now he had the certainty that the shapes he read about would not be shadows from dreamland much longer, and he felt rich in the promise of the book. The pictures rose before him as never before, flashing out like brilliant, many-colored suns from a mist that was golden and dancing with gold.

"What are you looking at?" he asked Niels.

Niels pointed to a portrait in his book representing Lassen, the hero of the Second of April.

"How ugly he is!" commented Erik.

"Ugly! Why he was a hero — would you call *him* ugly, too?" Niels turned the leaves back to the picture of a great poet.

"Awfully ugly!" replied Erik decisively, making a grimace. "What a nose! And look at the mouth, and the eyes, and those tufts around his head!"

Then Niels saw that he was ugly, and he was silenced. It had not occurred to him that greatness was not always cast in a mold of beauty.

"While I think of it," said Erik, closing his Spengler, "let me give you the key to the deck-house."

Niels would have brushed him aside gloomily, but Erik hung a small padlock key around his friend's neck on a broad piece of ribbon. "Shall we go down there?" he asked.

They went. Frithjof they found by the garden fence. He lay there eating green gooseberries, and had tears in his eyes because of the parting. Besides he was hurt that the others had not looked him up; for though he generally came uninvited, he felt that such a day demanded a certain amount of formality. Without speaking, he held out a handful of berries to them, but they had their favorite dishes for dinner, and turned up their noses.

"Sour!" said Erik with a shudder.

"Indigestible truck!" added Niels, disdainfully looking down at the proffered berries. "How can you eat it? Chuck the stuff, we're going down to the deck-house," and he pointed with his chin at the key, for his hands were in his pockets.

At that they all three set forth.

The deck-house was an old green-painted ship's cabin, which had once been bought at a beach auction. It had been put up by the fjord, and had served as a tool-house when the dam was being built, but now it was no longer in use. So the boys had taken possession of it, and concealed in it their ships, bows and arrows, leaping-poles, and other treasures, particularly such forbidden but indispensable things as powder, tobacco, and matches.

Niels opened the door of the deck-house with an air of gloomy solemnity. They went in and fumbled till they found their things in the dark corners of the empty bunks.

"Do you know," said Erik, with his head deep in a distant corner, "I'm going to blow mine up."

"Mine and Frithjof's too!" cried Niels with a grand, consecrating gesture.

"Not mine, by Joe!" exclaimed Frithjof; "then what'd we have to sail with when Erik's gone?"

"What indeed!" mocked Niels, turning away contemptuously.

Frithjof felt uncomfortable, but when the others had gone outside, he carefully moved his ship to a safer shelter.

Outside they quickly laid the powder in the ships imbedded in a nest of tarred oakum, set the sails, fixed the fuses, lighted them, and sprang back. Running along the beach, they signaled to the crew on board, loudly explaining to one another every chance turn of the ships as the result of the good captain's nautical skill. But the ships ran aground at the point without the desired explosion having taken place, and this gave Frithjof an opportunity nobly to sacrifice the wadding of his cap to the manufacture of new and better fuses.

With all sails set, the ships stood in toward Sjælland reef; the Britisher's huge frigates came heavily lurching in a closed ring, while the foam blew white around the black bows, and the cannon mounted at the head filled the air with their harsh clamor. Nearer and nearer — glowing with red and blue, glittering with gold, the figureheads of the *Albion* and the *Conqueror* rose fathom-high. Greyish masses of sails hid the horizon; the smoke rolled out in great white clouds, and drifted as a veiling mist low over the sun-bright glitter of the waves. Then the deck of Erik's ship was splintered with a feeble little puff; the oakum caught fire, a red blaze burst forth and ran along the spars, ate their way smoldering along the bolt-rope, then shot like long flashes of lightning into the sails, while the burning canvas shriveled up, broke, and flew in large black flakes far out to sea. The Danebrog was still waving high on the slender top of the tall schooner mast, the flagstaff was burned in two, the flag fluttered wildly like red wings eager for battle — but the flame caught it, and the smoke-blackened ship drifted without rudder or helmsman, dead and powerless, the sport of the winds and breakers. Niels's ship did not burn so well; the powder had caught fire and some smoke came out, but that was all, and it was not enough.

"Hey, there'" called Niels from the point, "sink her! Point the starboard cannon down the aft hatch and give her a volley!" He bent down and picked up a stone, "Ready, fire!" and the stone flew from his hand.

Erik and Frithjof followed suit, and soon the hull was in splinters. Then Erik's ship shared the same fate. The wreckage was hauled ashore to make a bonfire. It was piled up with dry seaweed and grass into a burning heap, from which thick smoke issued, while the crystals that hung on the seaweed burst and crackled with the intense heat.

For a long time the boys sat quietly around the bonfire, but suddenly Niels, still gloomy, jumped up and brought all his things from the deck-house, broke them into little bits, and threw them into the flames. Then Erik brought his, and Frithjof also brought some. The flames of the sacrificial pyre leaped so high that Erik was afraid they might be seen from the pasture, and began to smother them with wet seaweed, but Niels stood still, gazing sorrowfully after the smoke that drifted along the beach. Frithjof kept in the background and hummed to himself a heroic lay, which he accompanied secretly, now and then, with a sweeping, bardlike gesture, as if he were playing on the strings of an invisible harp.

At last the fire died down, and Erik and Frithjof went home, while Niels stayed behind to lock the deck-house. That done, he looked cautiously after the others, and then threw key and ribbon far out into the fjord. Erik happened to look around at that moment and saw them fall, but he quickly turned his head away, and began to run a race with Frithjof.

The next day he left.

*F*or a while they missed him sorely and bitterly, for their life had been gradually formed on the supposition that they were three to share it. Three were company, variety, change; two were boredom and nothing at all.

What in the word could two find to do?

Could two shoot at a target or two play ball? They could play Friday
and Robinson Crusoe, to be sure, but then who would be the savages?

Such Sundays! Niels was so very weary of existence that he began first
to review and afterwards, with the aid of Mr. Bigum's large atlas, to
extend his geographical knowledge far beyond the prescribed bounds.
Finally, he started to read the whole Bible through and to keep a diary.
But Frithjof, in his utter loneliness, stooped so low as to seek consolation in playing with his sisters.

After a while the past became less vivid to them, the longing less keen.
Sometimes on a quiet evening, when the sun reddened the walls in the
lonely chamber, and the distant, monotonous calling of the cuckoo died
down, making the stillness wider and larger, the longing would come
creeping into Niels's mind, stealing its power; but it no longer tortured,
it was a vague thing that lay lightly on him and was half sweet like a
pain that is passing.

His letters showed the same trend. In the beginning they were full of
regrets, questions, and wishes loosely strung together, but soon they grew
longer, dealt more with externals, narrated, and were written throughout
in a well-formed style that hid between the lines a certain conscious
pleasure in being able to write so well.

As time passed, many things that had not dared to show themselves
while Erik was there began to raise their heads. Imagination strewed its
bright flowers through the humdrum calm of an eventless life. A dream
atmosphere enveloped Niels's mind, bringing with it the provocative
fragrance of life, and, hidden in the fragrance, the insidious poison of
life-thirsting fancies.

So Niels grows up, and all the influences of his childhood work on
the plastic clay. Everything helps to shape it; everything is significant,
the real and the dreamed, what is known and what is foreshadowed —
all add their touch, lightly but surely, to that tracery of lines which is
destined to be first hollowed out and deepened and afterwards flattened
out and smoothed away.

Chapter VI

"Mr. Lyhne – Mrs. Boye; Mr. Frithjof Petersen – Mrs. Boye."

It was Erik who performed the introduction, and it took place in Mikkelsen's studio, a light, spacious room with a floor of stamped clay and a ceiling twenty-five feet high. At one end of the room two portals led to the yard; at the other, a series of doors opened into the smaller studios within. Everything was grey with the dust of clay and plaster and marble. It had made the cobweb threads overhead as thick as twine and had drawn river maps on the large windowpanes. It filled eyes and nose and mouth with outlined muscles, hair, and draperies on the medley of casts that filled the long shelves running round the room and made them look like a frieze from the destruction of Jerusalem. Even the laurels, high trees planted in big tubs in a corner near one of the portals, were powdered till they became greyer than grey olives.

Erik stood at his modeling in the middle of the studio wearing his blouse and with a paper cup on his dark, wavy hair. He had acquired a moustache and looked quite manly beside his two friends, who had just taken their bachelor's degree and, still pale and tired from their examinations, looked provincially proper with their too new clothes and their too closely cropped heads in rather large caps.

At a little distance from Erik's scaffolding, Mrs. Boye sat in a low high-backed chair, holding a richly bound book in one hand and a lump of clay in the other. She was small, quite small, and slightly brunette in coloring, with clear, light brown eyes. Her skin had a luminous whiteness, but in the shadows of the rounded cheek and throat it deepened to a dull golden tone which went well with the burnished hair of a dusky hue changing to a tawny blondness in the high lights.

She was laughing when they came in, as a child laughs – a long, merry peal, gleefully loud, delightfully free. Her eyes, too, had the artless gaze of a child, and the frank smile on her lips seemed all the more childlike because the shortness of her upper lip left the mouth slightly open revealing milk-white teeth.

But she was no child.

Was she a little and thirty? The fullness of the chin did not say "No," nor the ripe glow of the lower lip. Her figure was well rounded with firm, luxuriant outlines accentuated by the dark blue dress, which fitted snugly as a riding habit around her waist, arms, and bosom. A dull crimson silk kerchief lay in rich folds around her neck and over her shoulders, its ends tucked into the low pointed neck of her bodice. Carnations of the same color were fastened in her hair.

"I am afraid we interrupted a pleasant reading," said Frithjof with a glance at the richly bound book.

"No, indeed — not in the least. We had been quarreling for a full hour about what we read," replied Mrs. Boye. "Mr. Refstrup is a great idealist in everything that has to do with art, while I think it's dreadfully tiresome — all this about the crude reality that has to be purified and clarified and regenerated and what not until there is just pure nothingness left. Do me the favor of looking at that Bacchante of Mikkelsen's — the one which deaf Traffelini over there is cutting in marble. If I were to enter her in a descriptive catalogue . . . Good heavens! Number 77. A young lady in négligé is standing thoughtfully on both her feet and doesn't know what to do with a bunch of grapes. She should crush those grapes if I had my way — crush them till the red juice ran down her breast — now shouldn't she? Don't you agree with me?" and she caught Frithjof by the sleeve, almost shaking him in her childlike eagerness.

"Yes," Frithjof admitted; "yes, I do think there is something lacking — something of freshness — of spontaneity —"

"It's simply naturalness that's lacking, and good heavens, *why* can't we be natural? Oh, I know perfectly well; it's because we lack the courage. Neither the artists nor the poets are brave enough to own up to human nature as it is. Shakespeare was, though."

"Well, you know," came from Erik behind the figure he was modeling, "I never could get along very well with Shakespeare. It seems to me he does too much of it; he whirls you around till you don't know where you are."

"I shouldn't go so far as to say that," Frithjof demurred; "but on the other hand," he added with an indulgent smile, "I cannot call the berserker ragings of the great English poet by the name of conscious and intelligent artistic courage."

"Really? Gracious, how funny you are!" and she laughed till she was tired. She had risen and was strolling about the studio, but suddenly she turned, held out her arms toward Frithjof, and cried, "God bless you!" and laughed again until she was almost bent double.

Frithjof was on the verge of getting offended, but it seemed too fussy to go away angry, especially as he knew himself to be in the right, and moreover the lady was very pretty. So he stayed and began to talk to Erik, all the while trying for Mrs. Boye's benefit to infuse a tone of mature tolerance into his voice.

Meanwhile Mrs. Boye was roaming about at the other end of the studio, thoughtfully humming a tune, which sometimes rose in a few quick, laughing trills, then sank again into a slow, solemn recitative.

A head of the young Augustus was standing on a large packing case. She began to dust it. Then she found some clay and made moustaches, a pointed beard, and finally earrings, which she fastened on it.

While she was busy with this, Niels managed to stroll in her direction under cover of examining the casts. She had not glanced toward him once, but she must have sensed that he was there, for, without turning, she held out her hand to him and asked him to bring Erik's hat.

Niels put the hat into her outstretched hand, and she set it on the head of Augustus.

"Good old Shakespeareson," she said, patting the cheek of the travestied bust, "stupid old fellow who didn't know what he was doing! Did he just sit there and daub ink till he turned out a Hamlet head without thinking of it — did he?" She lifted the hat from the bust and passed her hand over the forehead in a motherly way as if she would push back its hair. "Lucky old chap, for all that! More than half lucky old poet boy! — For you must admit that he wasn't at all bad as a writer, this Shakespeare?"

"I confess I have my own opinion of that man," replied Niels, slightly vexed and blushing.

"Goodness gracious! Have you too got your own opinion about Shakespeare? Then what is your opinion? Are you for us or against us?" She struck an attitude by the side of the bust and stood there, smiling, with her arm resting on its neck.

"I am unable to say whether the opinion which you are astonished to learn I possess is so fortunate as to acquire significance from the fact of agreeing with your own, but I do think I may say that it is *for* you and your *protégé*. At any rate I hold the opinion that he knew what he was doing, weighed what he was doing, and dared it. Many a time he dared in doubt, and the doubt is still apparent. At other times he only half dared, and then he blurred over with new features that which he did not have courage to leave as he first had it."

And he went on in this strain.

While he was speaking, Mrs. Boye grew more and more restless. She looked nervously first to one side, then to the other, and drummed impatiently with her fingers, while her face clouded by a troubled look which finally deepened to one of pain.

At last she could contain herself no longer.

"Don't forget what you were going to say," she exclaimed, "but I implore you, Mr. Lyhne, stop doing that with your hand — that gesture as if you were pulling teeth! Please do, and don't let me interrupt you! Now I am all attention again, and I quite agree with you."

"But then it's of no use to say anymore."

"Why not?"

"When we agree?"

"When we agree!"

Neither of them meant anything in particular by these last words, but they said them in a significant tone, as if a world of delicate meanings were hidden in them, and looked at each other with a subtle smile, like an afterglow of the wit that had just flashed between them, while each wondered what the other meant and felt slightly annoyed at being so slow of comprehension.

They strolled back to the other end of the room, and Mrs. Boye took her seat on the low chair again.

Erik and Frithjof had talked till they were beginning to be bored with each other and were glad to be joined by the others. Frithjof approached Mrs. Boye and made himself agreeable, while Erik, with the modesty of the host, kept himself in the background.

"If I were curious," said Frithjof, "I should inquire what the book was that made you and Refstrup quarrel just as we were coming in."

"Do you inquire?"

"I do."

"Ergo?"

"Ergo!" replied Frithjof with a humble, acquiescent bow.

She held up the book and solemnly announced: *"Helge,* Oehlenschläger's *Helge.* – And what canto? It was The Mermaid visits King Helge.' – And what verse! It was the lines telling of how Tangkjaer lay down by Helge's side and how he couldn't control his curiosity any longer, but turned

– and at his side,
With white arms soft and round,
The greatest beauty he espied
That e'er on earth was found.

The maid had doffed her cloak of grey;
Her lovely limbs were bare,

Save for the robe like silver spray
That veiled her form so fair.

That is all he allows us to see of the mermaid's charms, and that is what I am dissatisfied with. I want a luxuriant, glowing picture there; I want to see something so dazzling that it takes my breath away. I want to be initiated into the mysterious beauty of such a mermaid body, and I ask of you, what can I make of lovely limbs with a piece of gauze spread over them? Good heavens! No, she should have been naked as a wave and with the wild lure of the sea about her. Her skin should have had something of the phosphorescence of the summer ocean and her hair something of the black, tangled horror of the seaweed. Am I not right? Yes, and a thousand tints of the water should come and go in the changeful glitter of her eyes. Her pale breast must be cool with a voluptuous coolness, and her limbs have the flowing lines of the waves. The power of the maelstrom must be in her kiss, and the yielding softness of the foam in the embrace of her arms."

She had talked herself into a glow, and stood there still animated by her theme, looking at her young listeners with large, inquiring child-eyes.

But they said nothing. Niels had flushed scarlet, and Erik looked extremely embarrassed. Frithjof was absolutely carried away and stared at her with the most open admiration, though of the three he was the one least aware how entrancingly beautiful she was, as she stood there with the glamour of her words about her.

Not many weeks had passed before Niels and Frithjof were as constant visitors in Mrs. Boye's home as Erik Refstrap. Besides her pale niece, they met a great many young people, coming poets, painters, actors, and architects, all artists by virtue of their youth rather than their talent, all full of hope, valiant, lusting for battle, and easily moved to enthusiasm. It is true, there were among them some of those quiet dreamers who bleat wistfully toward the faded ideals of the past; but most of them were full of ideas that were modern at the time, drunk with the theories of modernity, wild with its powers, dazzled by its clear morning light. They were modern, belligerently modern, modern to excess, and perhaps not the least because in their inmost hearts there was a strange, instinctive longing which had to be stifled, a longing which the new spirit could not satisfy — worldwide, all-embracing, all-powerful, and all-enlightening though it was.

But, for all that, the exultation of the storm was in their young souls. They had faith in the light of the great stars of thought; they had hope fathomless as the ocean. Enthusiasm bore them on the wings of the eagle, and their hearts expanded with the courage of thousands.

No doubt life would in time wear it all out, lull most of it to sleep; worldly wisdom would break down much, and cowardice would sweep away the rest — but what of it? The time that has gone with happiness does not come back with grief, and nothing the future may bring can wither a day or wipe out an hour in the life that has been lived.

To Niels the world, in those days, began to wear a different aspect. He heard his own vaguest, most secret thoughts loudly proclaimed by ten different mouths. He saw his own unique ideas, which to him had been a misty landscape, with lines blurred by fog, with unknown depths and muted notes — he saw this landscape unveiled in the bright, clear, sharp colors of day, revealed in every detail, furrowed everywhere by roads, and with people swarming on the roads. There was something strangely unreal in the very fact that the creations of his fancy had become so real.

He was no longer a lonely child-king, reigning over lands that his own dreams had conjured up. No, he was one of a crowd, a man in an army, a soldier in the service of modern ideas. A sword had been placed in his hand, and a banner waved before him.

What a wonderful time full of promise! And how strange to hear with his ears the indistinct, mysterious whisper of his soul now sounding through the air of reality like wild, challenging trumpet blasts, like the thunder of battering rams against temple walls, like the whizzing of David's pebble against Goliath's brow, like exultant fanfares. It was as though he heard himself speaking, with strange tongues, with a clarity and power not his own, about that which belonged to his deepest, innermost self.

This gospel of modernity, with its message of dissolution and perfection, did not sound only from the lips of his contemporaries. There were older men with names that carried weight whose eyes were likewise open to the glories of new ideas. These men used more pompous words and had more magnificent conceptions; the names of past centuries swept along in their train; history was with them — the history of the world and the human mind, the Odyssey of thought. These were men who in their youth had been moved by the very things that now thrilled the young people and had borne witness to the spirit within them; but when they heard in their own voices the sound which tells a man crying in the wilderness that he is alone, they were silenced. The young people, however, remembered only that these men had spoken, not that they had been silent; they were ready to bring laurel wreaths and martyr crowns, willing to admire and happy in their admiration. Nor did the objects of their homage repel this late-born appreciation; they put on the crowns in good faith, looked at themselves in a large and historic light, and poetized out of their past the less heroic features; as for the old conviction, which ill winds had cooled, they soon talked it into a glow again.

Niels Lyhne's family in Copenhagen, more particularly the old Councilor Neergaards, were not at all pleased with the circle their young relative had entered. It was not the modern ideas that worried them, but rather the fact that some of the young men found long hair, great hunting boots, and a slight slovenliness favorable to the growth of such ideas, and though Niels himself was not at all fanatical on this point, it was annoying to meet him, and even more annoying to have their friends meet him, in company with youths who could be thus characterized. These things, however, were trifles compared to his intimacy with Mrs. Boye and his frequenting the theater in company with her and her pale niece.

Not that there was anything in particular to be said against Mrs. Boye, but people talked about her. They said a great many things.

She was well born, a Konneroy, and the Konneroys were among the oldest, most finely patrician families in town. Yet she had broken with them. Some said it was on account of a dissipated brother, whom they had sent off to the colonies to get rid of him. Certain it was that the break was complete, and there were even whispers that old Konneroy had cursed her, and afterwards had had an attack of his bad spring asthma.

All this had happened after she became a widow.

Mr. Boye, her husband, had been a pharmaceutist, an *assessor pharmacia*, and had been knighted. When he died he was sixty and owned a barrel and a half of gold. So far as anyone knew, they had lived quite happily together. In the first three years of their marriage, the elderly husband had been very much in love, but later they had each lived their own life, he busy with his garden and with keeping up his reputation as a great man at stag parties, she with theaters, romantic music, and German poetry.

Then he died.

When the year of mourning was over, the widow went to Italy and lived there for two or three years, spending most of the time in Rome. There was nothing in the rumor that she had smoked opium in the French club, nor in the story that she had allowed herself to be modeled in the same manner as Paulina Borghese; and the little Russian prince who shot himself while she was in Naples did not commit suicide for her sake. It was true, however, that German artists never tired of serenading her; and it was true that one morning she had donned the dress of an Albanian peasant girl and had seated herself on the steps of a church high up in the Via Sistina, where a newly arrived artist had engaged her to stand as a model for him with a pitcher on her head and a little brown boy holding her hand. At least there was such a picture hanging on her wall.

On the way home from Italy she met a countryman, a noted clever critic, who would rather have been a poet. A negative, skeptical nature, people called him, a keen mind, one who dealt harshly and pitilessly with others because he dealt harshly and pitilessly with himself and supposed his brutality to be justified by that fact. Nevertheless, he was not quite what they believed him to be; he was not so repellently uncompromising nor so robustly consistent as he appeared. Although he was always in a state of strife against the idealistic tendencies of the age and called them by more disparaging names, still he felt drawn toward these dreamy, ethereal ideals, this blue, blue-mist mysticism, these unattainable heights and evanescent lights; they appealed to him more than the earthborn opinions for which he did battle and in which, most of the time, he believed.

Rather against his will, he fell in love with Mrs. Boye, but he did not tell her so, for his was not a young and open love, nor a hopeful one. He loved her as a creature of another, a finer and happier race than his own, and there was in his love a rancor, an instinctive rage against everything in her that bore the marks of race.

He looked with hostile, jealous eyes upon her sentiments and opinions, her tastes and views of life. He fought with every weapon he possessed, with subtle eloquence, with heartless logic and harsh authority, with derision wrapped in pity, to bring her over to his side, and he won. But when truth had conquered, and she had become like him, he saw that the victory was too complete, that he had loved her as she was, with her illusions and prejudices, her dreams and her errors, and not as she had now become. Dissatisfied with himself, with her and with everything in his own country, he went away and did not return. But then she had just begun to love him.

This relationship, of course, gave people food for talk, and they made the most of it. The Councilor's wife told Niels about it in the tone that aged virtue uses in speaking of young error, but Niels took it in a manner that offended and horrified the old lady. He replied in a high strain about the tyranny of society and the freedom of the individual, about the plebeian respectability of the mob and the nobility of passion.

From that day on he went but seldom to the home of his solicitous relatives, but Mrs. Boye saw him all the more frequently.

Chapter VII

*I*t was an evening in spring; the sun threw a red light into the room, as it sank toward the horizon. The wings of the windmill on the embankment drew shadows over the windowpanes and the walls, coming, going, in a monotonous swinging from darkness to light: a moment of darkness, two moments of light.

At the window, Niels Lyhne sat gazing through the darkly burnished elms on the embankment to the fiery clouds beyond. He had been in the country, walking under blossoming beeches, past green rye fields, over flower-decked meadows. Everything had been so fair and light, the sky so blue, the Sound so bright, the women he met so wondrously beautiful. Singing, he had followed the forest path, but soon the words had died out of his song, then the rhythm was lost, at last the tones were muted, and silence came over him like a fit of giddiness. He closed his eyes, and still he felt how his body drank the light, and his nerves vibrated with it. Every breath he drew of the cool, intoxicating air sent his blood rushing more wildly through the quivering, helpless veins. He felt as though all the teeming, budding, growing, germinating forces of spring were mysteriously striving to vent themselves through him in a mighty cry, and he thirsted for this cry, listened for it, till his listening grew into a vague, turgid longing.

Now, as he sat there by the window, the longing awoke in him again.

He yearned for a thousand tremulous dreams, for cool and delicate images, transparent tints, fleeting scents, and exquisite music from streams of highly strung, tensely drawn silvery strings — and then silence, the innermost heart of silence, where the waves of air never bore a single stray tone, but where all was rest unto death, steeped in the calm glow of red colors and the languid warmth of fiery fragrance. — This was not what he longed for, but the images glided forth from his mood and submerged all else until he turned from them to follow his own train of thought again.

He was weary of himself, of cold ideas and brain dreams. Life a poem? Not when you went about forever poetizing about your own life instead of living it. How innocuous it all was, and empty, empty, empty! This chasing after yourself, craftily observing your own tracks — in a circle, of course. This sham diving into the stream of life while all the time you sat angling after yourself, fishing yourself up in one curious disguise or another! If he could only be overwhelmed by something — life, love, passion — so that he could no longer shape it into poems, but had to let it shape him!

Involuntarily he made a gesture as if to ward it off with his hand. After all, he was afraid in his inmost heart of this mighty thing called passion. This storm wind sweeping away everything settled and authorized and acquired in humanity as if it were dead leaves. He did not like it! This roaring flame squandering itself in its own smoke — no, *he* wanted to burn slowly.

And yet this living on at half speed in quiet waters, always in sight of land, seemed so paltry. Would that the storm and waves would come! If he only knew how, his sails should fly to the yards for a merry run over the Spanish Main of life! Farewell to the slowly dripping days, farewell to the pleasant little hours! Peace be with you, you dull moods that have to be furbished with poetry before you can shine, you lukewarm emotions that have to be clothed in warm dreams and yet freeze to death! May you go to your own place! I am headed for a coast where sentiments twine themselves like luxuriant vines around every fiber of the heart — a rank forest; for every vine that withers, twenty are in blossom; for each one that blossoms, a hundred are in bud.

Oh, that I were there!

He grew tired of his longing and sick of himself. He needed people. But of course, Erik was not in now. Frithjof had been with him all morning, and it was too late for the theater. Nevertheless he went out and strolled dejectedly through the streets.

Perhaps Mrs. Boye would be in. This was not one of her evenings and it was rather late. Suppose he try, anyway.

Mrs. Boye was in. She was at home alone. Too tired from the spring air to go to a dinner party with her niece, she had preferred to lie on the sofa, drinking strong tea and reading Heine; but now she was tired of verses and wanted to play lotto.

So they played lotto. Fifteen, twenty, thirty-seven, a long series of figures, the rattling of dice in a bag, and an irritating sound of balls rolling on the floor in the apartment above them. . . .

"This is not amusing," said Mrs. Boye, when they had played for a long time without covering any numbers. "Is it? — No!" she answered herself and shook her head disconsolately. "But what else can we play?"

She folded her hands before her on the disks and looked at Niels with a hopeless, inquiring gaze.

Niels really did not know.

"Anything but music!" She bent her face down over her hands and touched her lips to the knuckles, one after the other, the whole row, then back again. "This is the most wretched existence in the world," she said, looking up. "It isn't possible to have anything like an adventure, and the small happenings that life has to offer are surely not enough to keep one's spirits up. Don't you feel that, too?"

"Well I can't suggest anything better than that we act like the Caliph in Arabian Nights. With that silk kimono you are wearing, if you would only wind a white cloth around your head, and let me have your large Indian shawl, we could easily pass for two merchants from Mossul."

"And what should we two unfortunate merchants do?"

"Go down to Storm bridge, hire a boat for twenty pieces of gold, and sail up the dark river."

"Past the sand chests?"

"Yes, with colored lamps on the masthead."

"Like Ganem, the Slave of Love. — Oh, I know that line of thought so well! It's exactly like a man — to get so terribly busy building up scenery and background, forgetting the action itself for the setting. Have you never noticed that women live much less in their imagination than men? We don't know how to taste pleasure in our fancy or escape from pain with a fanciful consolation. What is, is. Imagination — it is so innocuous. When we get as old as I am now, then sometimes we content ourselves with the poverty-stricken comedy of imagination. But we ought never to do it — never I

She settled herself languidly on the sofa, half reclining her hand under her chin, her elbow supported by the cushions. She gazed dreamily out before her, and seemed quite lost in melancholy thoughts.

Niels was silent too, and the room was so quiet that the restless hopping of the canary bird was plainly heard; the great clock ticked and ticked its way through the silence, louder and louder, and a string in the open piano, suddenly vibrating, emitted a long, low dying note that blended with the softly singing stillness.

She looked very young as she lay there, flooded from head to foot in the soft yellow light of the lamp above her. There was something alluring in the incongruity of her beautiful, strongly molded throat and matronly Charlotte Corday cap with the frank child eyes and the little mouth opening over milk-white teeth.

Niels looked at her admiringly.

"How strange it is to long for one's self!" she said; "and yet I often, so often, long for myself as a young girl. I love her as one whom I had been very close to and shared life and happiness and everything with, and then had lost while I stood helpless. What a wonderful time that was! You cannot conceive the purity and delicacy of such a young girl's soul when she is just beginning to love for the first time. It can only be told in music, but you can think of it as a festival in a fairy palace, where the air shines like bluish silver. It is filled with cool flowers, and they change color, their tints are slowly shifting. Everything is song, jubilant and yet soft. Dim presentiments gleam and glow like mystic wine in exquisite dream goblets. It is all song and fragrance; a thousand scents are wafted through the palace. Oh, I could weep when I think of it, and when I think that if it could all come back to me, by a miracle, just as it was, it would no longer bear me up; I should fall through like a cow trying to dance on cobwebs."

"No, quite the contrary," said Niels eagerly, and his voice trembled, as he went on: "no, the love you could feel now would be much finer, much more spiritual than that young girl's."

"Spiritual! I hate this spiritual love. The flowers growing from that soil are made of cotton cloth; they don't even grow, they are taken from the head and stuck in the heart, because the heart has no flowers of its own. That is exactly what I envy in the young girl: everything about her is genuine, she does not fill the goblet of her love with the makeshift of imagination. Do not suppose, because her love is shot through and shadowed over by imagined pictures and again pictures in a great, teeming vagueness, that she cares more for those images than for the earth she walks upon. It is only that all her senses and instincts and powers are reaching out for love everywhere — everywhere, without ever feeling weary. But she does not revel in her fancies, nor even so much as rest in them; no, she is very much more genuine, so genuine that in her own unwitting manner she very often becomes innocently cynical. You have no idea, for instance, of what intoxicating pleasure a young girl finds in breathing secretly the odor of cigars that clings to the clothes of the man she loves — that is a thousand times more to her than a whole conflagration of fancies. I despise imagination. What good is it, when our whole being yearns toward the heart of another, to be admitted only to the chilly anteroom of his imagination! And that is what happens so often. How often we have to submit to letting the man we love deck us out with his imagination, put a halo around our head, tie wings on our shoulders, and wrap us in a star-spangled robe! Then at last he finds us worthy of his love, when we masquerade in this costume; but then we can't be ourselves, because we are too dressed up, and because men confuse us by kneeling in the dust and worshiping us instead of just taking us as we are and simply loving us."

Niels was quite bewildered. He had picked up the handkerchief she dropped and sat there intoxicating himself with its perfume. He was not at all prepared to have her look at him in that impatient, questioning way, just as he was absorbed in studying her hand, but he managed to answer that he thought a man could not give a finer proof of his love than this — that he had to justify himself to himself for loving a human being so unutterably, and therefore set her so high and surrounded her with a nimbus of divinity.

"But that is just what I find so insulting," said Mrs. Boye, "as if we were not divine enough in ourselves."

Niels smiled complacently.

"No, you mustn't smile, I'm not joking. It is really very serious, for this adoration is at bottom tyrannical in its fanaticism; it cramps us in a mold of man's ideal. Slash a heel and clip a toe! Anything in us that doesn't square with man's conception has to be eliminated, perhaps not by force, but by ignoring it, systematically relegating it to oblivion, and never giving it a chance to develop, while the qualities we don't possess or that aren't in the least characteristic of us are forced to the rankest growth by lauding them to the skies, taking for granted that we have them in the fullest measure, and making them the cornerstone on which man builds his love. I say that we are subjected to a drill; a man's love puts us through a drill. And we submit to it, even those who love no one submit to it, contemptible minions that we are!"

She had risen from her reclining posture and looked threateningly at Niels.

"If I were beautiful! — oh, I mean ravishingly beautiful, more alluring than any woman who ever lived, so that all who saw me were struck with unquenchable, agonizing love as by witchcraft — then I would use the power of my beauty to make them adore *me*, not then: traditional bloodless ideal, but myself, as I am, every inch, every line of *my* being, every gleam of *my* nature!"

She had risen now to her full height, and Niels thought he ought to go, but he stood turning over in his mind a great many audacious words, which, after all, he did not dare to utter. At last, summoning all his courage, he seized her hand and kissed it, but she gave him her other hand to kiss too, and then he could say nothing more than: "Good night."

Niels Lyhne had fallen in love with Mrs. Boye, and he was happy because of it.

When he went home through the same streets where he had strolled so dejectedly that same evening, it seemed to him that ages had passed since he walked there. His bearing had acquired a new poise, a grave decorum, and when he carefully buttoned his gloves, he did so with a

subconscious sense that he had undergone a great change which somehow demanded that he should button his gloves — carefully.

Too much absorbed to think of sleep, he went up on the embankment.
It seemed to him that his thoughts flowed very quietly.

He was surprised at his own calm, but he did not have perfect faith
in it. He felt as though something in the very depths of his being were
bubbling, very softly, but persistently: welling up, seething, pressing on,
but far, far away. He was in a mood as one who waits for something
that must come from afar, a distant music that must draw near, little
by little, singing, murmuring, frothing, rushing, roaring, and whirling
down over him, catching him up he knew not how, carrying him he
knew not whither, coming on as a flood, breaking as a surf, and then —

But now he was calm. There was only the tremulous singing in the
distance; otherwise all was peace and tranquility.

He loved — he said it aloud to himself again and again. The words
had such a strange ring of dignity, and held such deep meanings. They
meant that he was no longer a captive in the imagined world of his
childhood, nor was he the sport of aimless longings and misty dreams.
He had escaped from the elf land that had grown up with him and
around him, encircling him with a hundred arms, blindfolding him
with a hundred hands. He had broken away from its grasp and bad
become master of himself, and though it reached after him, implored
him with dumb appealing eyes, and beckoned him with white fluttering
garments, its power was dead as a dream killed by day, a mist dispelled
by the sun. Was not his young love day and sun and all the world? He
had been strutting about in a royal purple not yet spun, and had taken
his seat on a throne not yet built; but now he stood on a high mountain,
looking out over the world that stretched before him like a plain. In
this world thirsting for song he had as yet no existence and was not
even awaited. What a rapturous thought it was that, in all this silent,
wakeful infinity, not a breath of his spirit had stirred a leaf or raised a
ripple. It was all his to win, and he knew that he could win it. He felt
strong and all-conquering as only those can feel whose songs are still
unsung, throbbing in their own breast.

The soft spring air was full of perfumes, not saturated with them as
the summer nights may be, but rather as it were streaked — now with
the pungent aroma from resinous young poplars, now with the cool
breath of late violets, and again with the sweet almond odor of cherry
trees. The scents came and mingled, were wafted away and dissolved;
sometimes one would quicken and free itself from the others, only to
die as suddenly or to vanish slowly on a breath of wind. Light moods
flitted across his mind like the shadows from this fitful dance of scents,
and as the perfumes mocked his senses by coming and going as they

listed, so his mind was baffled by his vain longing to be borne aloft, calmly resting in tranquil flight on the slowly gliding wings of a mood. For his moods were not yet birds with wings strong enough to carry him; they were down and feathers only, drifting on the wind, falling like snow, and melting.

He tried to recall the picture of her as she lay on the sofa and talked to him, but it would not come. He saw her vanishing in a lane of trees; or sitting and reading with her hat on, holding one of the large white leaves in her gloved fingers, just on the point of turning it, then turning leaf after leaf. He saw her entering her carriage in the evening after the theater and nodding to him behind the pane; then the carriage drove away, and he stood looking after it; it kept on driving, and he still followed it with his eyes. Indifferent faces came and spoke to him, figures he had not seen for years passed down the street, turned and looked after him, and still the carriage kept on driving, and he could not get rid of it, could not think of other pictures because of that carriage. Then, just as he was getting nervous with impatience, it came: the yellow light from the lamp, the eyes, the mouth, the hand under the chin, as plainly as if it were all before him there in the darkness.

How lovely she was, how mild, how fair! He loved her with a desire that knelt at her feet, begging for all this seductive beauty. Cast yourself from your throne down to me! Make yourself my slave! Put the chain around your neck with your own hands, but not in sport — I want to pull the chain, I demand submission in your every limb, bondage in your eyes! Oh, that I could draw you to me with a love philter, but, no, a love philter would compel you, you would yield to its power without volition, and I want none to be your master but myself. Your will must be broken in your hands, and you must hold it out humbly to me. You shall be my queen, and I your slave, but my slave's foot must be on your queenly neck. There is no lunacy in this desire, for is it not in the nature of a woman's love to be proud and strong and to bend? It is love, I know, to be weak and to reign.

He felt that he could never draw to himself the part of her soul that was one with the luxuriant, glowing, sensuous-soft aspect of her beauty; it would never clasp him in those gleaming Juno arms, never in passionate weakness give that voluptuous neck to his kisses — never in all eternity. He saw it all clearly. He could win, perhaps he already had won, the young girl in her, and he was sure that she, the full-blooded beauty, felt this fair young creature who had died within her mysteriously stirring in her living grave to clasp him with slender maiden arms and meet him with timid maiden lips. But his love was not like that. He loved the very thing in her that he could not win, loved this neck with its warm, flowerlike whiteness gleaming with a dew of gold under the dusky sky. He sobbed with yearning passion and wrung his hands with impotent desire, threw his arms around a tree, leaned his cheek against the bark, and wept.

Chapter VIII

*T*here was in Niels Lyhne's nature a lame reflectiveness, child of an instinctive shrinking from decisive action, grandchild of a subconscious sense that he lacked personality. He was always struggling against this reflectiveness, sometimes goading himself by calling it vile names, then again decking it out as a virtue that was a part of his inmost self and was bound up with all his possibilities and powers. But whatever he made of it, and however he looked upon it, he hated it as a secret infirmity, which he might perhaps hide from the world, but never from himself; it was always there to humiliate him whenever he was alone with himself. How he envied the audacity that rushes confidently into words, never heeding that words bring actions, and actions bring consequences — until those consequences are at its heels. People who possessed it always seemed to him like centaurs — man and horse cast in a single mold. With them impulse and leap were one, whereas he was divided into rider and horse — impulse one thing, leap something very different.

Whenever he pictured himself declaring his love for Mrs. Boye — and he always had to picture everything — he could plainly see himself in the scene, his attitude, his every motion, his whole figure from the front, from the side, and from the back. He could see himself falter with the feverish irresolution that robbed him of his presence of mind and paralyzed him, while he stood there awaiting her answer as if it were a blow forcing him to his knees, instead of a shuttlecock to be thrown back in ever so many ways and returned in as many more.

He thought of speaking, and he thought of writing, but he never managed simply to blurt it out. It was only in veiled declarations and in a half-feigned lyric passion that made a pose of being carried away into hot words and fantastic hopes. Nevertheless, a certain intimacy of a strange kind grew up between them, born of a youth's humble love, a dreamer's ardent longing, and a woman's pleasure in being the inaccessible object of romantic desire. Their relation took the form of a myth that arose, neither of them knew how, a pale, still myth bred in a drawing room. Its heroine was a fair woman who had loved in her early youth one of the great men in the world of thought. He had gone away to die in a strange land, forgotten and forsaken. And the fair woman sat sorrowing for many long years, though none knew her suffering; solitude alone was sacred enough to look upon her grief. Then came a youth who called the departed great one master, who was filled with his spirit and enthusiastic for his work. And he loved the sorrowing woman. To her it seemed that the dead happy days rose from their grave and came to life again. A sweet, strange bewilderment came over her; past and present were blurred in the silvery mist of a shadowy dream-day, in which she loved the youth, partly as himself and partly as the image of another, and gave him the half of her soul. But he must tread softly, lest the dream-bubble should burst; he must put a stern bar to all hot earthly longings, lest they should dispel the tender twilight and wake her to sorrow again.

Sheltered by this myth, their intimacy gradually took on a stable form. They called each other by their Christian names and were Niels and Tema to each other when they were alone, while the presence of the niece was reduced to a minimum. To be sure, Niels sometimes tried to break through the accepted barriers, but Mrs. Boye was so much the stronger that she could easily and gently quell all such attempts at insubordination, and Niels had to submit and fall back for a time on this fanciful passion with real tableaux. Their relation never ran out into a platonic flatness; nor did it sink to rest in the monotony of habit. Rest was the word that least of all described it. Niels Lyhne's hope was never weary, and though it was gently suppressed whenever it would flare up in a demand, that only made it smolder more hotly than ever in secret. And how Mrs. Boye would feed the fire by her thousand and one coquetries, her provocative simplicity, and her naked courage in discussing the most delicate subjects! Besides, the game was not entirely in her hands, for there were times when her blood would dream in its idleness of rewarding this half-tamed devotion by lavishing on it the fullest rapture of love in order to rejoice in its wondering happiness. But such a dream was not easily extinguished, and the next time Niels came she would meet him with the nervousness of conscious sin, a shyness born of wrongdoing, a sweet shame that made the air strangely tremulous with passion.

There was yet another thing that gave their intimacy a certain tension. Niels Lyhne's love possessed so much virility that he chivalrously held himself back from taking in imagination what the reality denied him, and even in that separate world where everything did his bidding he respected Mrs. Boye as if she were actually present.

Hence their relation was well buttressed from both sides, and there was no immediate danger that it would fall to pieces. Indeed, it seemed made for a nature at once brooding and athirst for life such as Niels Lyhne's, and though it was only a game, it was a game of realities, sufficient to give him that undercurrent of passion which he needed.

Niels Lyhne was bent upon being a poet, and there was much in the external circumstances of his life to lead his thoughts in that direction and stimulate his faculties for the task. So far, however, he had little but his dreams to write about, and nowhere is there more sameness and monotony than in the world of imagination; for in that dreamland, which seems so boundless and so infinitely varied, there are, in fact, only a few short beaten paths where everybody walks and from which no one ever strays. People may differ, but in their dreams they do not differ; there they always attain the three or four things that they desire — it may be with more or less speed and completeness, but they always attain them in the end. No one seriously dreams of himself as empty-handed. Therefore no one ever discovers himself in his dreams or becomes conscious through them of his individuality. Our dreams tell nothing of how we are satisfied when we win the treasure, how we relinquish it when lost, how we feast on it while it is ours, where we turn when it is taken from us.

Niels Lyhne's poetry had hitherto been nothing but the expression of an esthetic personality which, in a general way, found spring teeming, the ocean wide, love erotic, and death melancholy. He himself was not in his poems; he merely put the verses together. But now a change came over him. Now that he wooed a woman and wanted her to love him — him, Niels Lyhne of Lönborggaard, who was twenty-three years old, walked with a slight stoop, had beautiful hands and small ears, and was a little timid, wanted her to love him and not the idealized Nicolaus of his dreams, who had a proud bearing and confident manners, and was a little older — now he began to take a vital interest in this Niels whom he had hitherto walked about with as a slightly unpresentable friend. He had been so busy decking himself with the qualities he lacked that he had not had time to take note of those he possessed, but now he began to piece his own self together from scattered memories and impressions of his childhood and from the most vivid moments of his life. He saw with pleased surprise how it all fitted together, bit by bit, and was welded into a much more familiar personality than the one he had chased after in his dreams. This figure was far more genuine, far stronger, and more richly endowed. It was no mere dead stump of an ideal, but a living thing, full of infinite shifting possibilities playing through it and shaping it to a thousandfold unity. Good God, he *had* powers that could be used just as they were! He *was* Aladdin, and there was not a thing he had been storming the clouds for but it had fallen right down into his turban.

Now came a happy time for Niels, the glorious time when the mighty impulse of growth sweeps us jubilantly past the dead points in our own nature; when we are filled to bursting with a strength that makes us eager to put our shoulders to mountains if need be, while we build away bravely on the Tower of Babel, which is meant to pierce the sky, but ends in being just a squatty structure that we go on all our lives adding to — now a timid spire, now a freakish bay window.

Everything was changed; his nature, his faculties, and his work fitted into one another like cogged wheels. He could never think of stopping to rejoice in his art, for a thing was no sooner finished than it was cast aside; he had outgrown it even while he worked on it, and it became a mere step that led upward to an ever-receding goal, one of many steps on a road he had left behind him and forgotten even while it resounded with his footfall.

While he felt himself borne along by new impulses and new thoughts to greater power and wider vision, he grew more and more solitary. One after another of his old friends and comrades fell back and vanished from his ken, for he lost interest in them when he saw less and less difference between these men of the opposition and that majority which they attacked. Everything seemed to him to melt together in one great hostile mass of boredom. What did they write when they gave the call to battle? Pessimistic verses in which they declared that dogs were often more faithful than men and jailbirds more honest than those who walked freely about, eloquent odes to the effect that green woods and brown heath were preferable to dusty cities, stories of peasant virtue and rich men's vice, of red-blooded nature and anemic civilization, the narrowness of age and the divine right of youth. What modest demands they made when they wrote! They were at least bolder when they talked within four safe walls.

No, when his time came, he would give them music — a clarion call!

His older friendships suffered too, especially that with Frithjof. The fact was that Frithjof, who had a very positive nature, a good head for systems, and a broad back for dogmas, had read a little too much Heiberg, and had taken it all for gospel truth, never suspecting that the makers of systems are clever folk who fashion their systems from their books and not their books from their systems. It is a well-known fact that young people who have committed themselves to a system generally become great dogmatists, because of the praiseworthy affection youth often bears to what is finished and finite. And when you have become the possessor of the whole truth, it would be unpardonable to keep it for yourself alone and to allow less fortunate fellow creatures to go their own misguided way, instead of leading and instructing them, pruning away their wild shoots with loving severity, forcing them up against the wall with gentle coercion, and pointing out to them the lines along which they must grow, in order that they may sometime, when they have been formed into correct and artistic espaliers, thank you, even if tardily, for the trouble you have taken.

Niels was fond of saying that he liked nothing better than criticism, but the truth was that he preferred admiration, and he certainly would not brook criticism from Frithjof, whom he had always regarded as his serf, and who had always been delighted to wear the livery of his opinions and his principles. And here he was trying to play the equal and to masquerade in a self-chosen mantle! Of course he must be snubbed, and Niels first tried, in a tone of good-natured superiority, to make Frithjof ridiculous in his own eyes, but when that would not work he had recourse to insolent paradoxes, which he would scorn to discuss, simply throwing them out in all their grotesque hideousness and then retiring behind a teasing silence.

In this way, they grew apart.

With Erik he got on better. Their boyish friendship had always kept a certain reserve, a kind of spiritual modesty, and this had saved them from the too great familiarity that is so dangerous to friendship. They had been enthusiastic together in the festival hall of their souls and had chatted intimately in the drawing room, but they had never made free with each other's bedrooms, bathrooms, and other private places in the mansion of their souls.

It was the same now; indeed, the reserve was, if anything, stricter, at least on Niels's part, but that did not lessen their friendship, the cornerstone of which, now as of old, was Niels Lyhne's admiration for Erik's spirit and audacity, his way of seeming at home with life, and his readiness to grasp and hold. Yet Niels could not conceal from himself that the friendship was extremely one-sided. Not that Erik was wanting in real affection or faith in him — far from it. No one could think more highly of Niels than Erik did; he considered him so vastly his own superior in intellect that he never dreamed of criticizing, but this blind admiration led him to place Niels and his work and interests too far beyond the horizon his own eyes could scan. He was sure that Niels would go far along the road he had chosen, but he was equally sure that his own feet had nothing to do on that path, nor did he ever attempt to set them there.

Niels felt that this was rather hard; for though Erik's ideals were not his, and though Erik in his art tried to express a romanticism or a romantic sentimentalism with which he was not in accord, he could still feel a broader sympathy by virtue of which he faithfully followed his friend's development, rejoiced with him when he gained a step, and helped him to hope when he stood still.

In this way their friendship was one-sided, and it was not strange that Niels should have his eyes opened to the lack in it just at the time when his own mind was struggling with new ideas, and he felt the need of pouring out his thoughts to a sympathetic listener. It made him bitter, and he began to examine more closely this friend whom he had always judged so leniently. A dreary sense of loneliness came over him as he realized how everything he had brought with him from home and from the old days seemed to fall away from him and let him go his own way, forgotten and forsaken. The door to the past was barred, and he stood outside, empty-handed and alone; whatever he needed and desired he must win for himself — new friends and new shelter, new affections and new memories.

*F*or more than a year Mrs. Boye had been Niels's only real companion, when a letter from his mother, telling him that his father was dangerously ill, called him back to Lönborggaard.

When he arrived, his father was dead.

The consciousness that for several years he had longed very little for his home weighed on Niels almost like a crime. He had often enough visited it in his thoughts, but always as a guest with the dust of other lands on his clothes and the memories of other places in his heart; he had never longed for it in passionate homesickness as for the fair sanctuary of his life, nor pined to kiss its soil and rest under its roof. Now he repented that he had been faithless to his home, and, oppressed as he was by his grief, he felt his remorse darkened by a sense that in some mysterious way he was an accessory to what had happened, as though his faithlessness had called death in. He wondered how he could ever have lived contentedly away from his home which now drew him with such strange power. With every fiber of his being he clung to it, in an infinite desolate longing, uneasy because he could not become one with it as fully as he would, miserable because the thousand memories that called from every corner and every bush, from sounds and myriad scents, from the play of light and from the silence itself — because all these things called with such distant voices that he could not grasp them in the strength and fullness he craved; they seemed only to whisper in his soul like the rustling of leaves that fall to the ground and the lapping of waves that flow on and ever on. . . .

Happy in his sorrow is he who at the death of one dear to him can weep all his tears over the emptiness, the desolation, and the loneliness. Sorer and bitterer are the tears with which you try to atone for the past when you have failed in love toward one who is gone and to whom you can never make amends for what you have sinned. For now they come back to you: not only the hard words, the subtly poisoned retorts, the harsh censure, and the unreasoning anger, but even unkind thoughts that were not put into words, hasty judgments that merely passed through your mind, unseen shruggings of the shoulder, and hidden smiles full of contempt and impatience, they all come back like malign arrows, sinking their barb deep in your own breast, their dull barb, for the point has been broken off in the heart that is no more. There is nothing you can expiate anymore, nothing. Now there is abundance of love in your heart, now that it is too late. Go now to the cold grave with your full heart! Does it bring you any nearer? Plant flowers and bind wreaths — does that help you?

At Lonborggaard they were binding wreaths; there too, they were haunted by memories of hours when love had been silenced by harsher voices; to them, too, the stern lines about the closed mouth of the grave spoke of remorse.

It was a dark, sad time, but it held a ray of light in that it brought mother and son more closely together than they had been for many, many years; for in spite of the great love they bore to each other, they had always been, and were, on their guard each toward the other, and there had been a certain reserve in their relationship, from the time when Niels grew too large to sit on his mother's knee. He had shrunk from the excitable and high-strung side of her nature, while she had felt something alien in the timidity and hesitation of his. But now life itself, which keys up and tones down and harmonizes, had prepared their hearts, and would soon give them wholly to each other.

Scarcely two months after the funeral, Mrs. Lyhne fell violently ill, and for a long time her life was in danger. The anxiety that filled these weeks seemed to force their earlier grief into the background, and when Mrs. Lyhne began to get better, it seemed to both her and Niels that years had been thrust in between them and the freshly made grave. Especially to Mrs. Lyhne the time seemed long. While she was ill she had been sure that she was going to die and had been very much afraid of death. Even now that she had begun to recover, and the doctor had declared the danger to be past, she could not rid herself of her gloomy thoughts.

It was a dreary convalescence, in which her strength returned as it seemed reluctantly, drop by drop. She felt no gentle and healing drowsiness, but rather a restless languor with a depressing sense of weakness and an incessant, impotent longing for strength.

After a while there was a change; her recovery was more rapid, and her strength came back. Still the idea that she and life were soon to part did not leave her, but lay like a shadow over her and held her captive in a perturbed and yearning melancholy.

One evening she was sitting alone in the summer parlor, gazing out through the wide-open doors. The trees of the garden hid the gold and crimson of the sunset, but in one spot the trunks parted to reveal a bit of fiery sky, from which a sunburst of long, deep golden rays shot out, waking green tints and bronze-brown reflections in the dark leafy masses.

High above the restless treetops, the clouds drifted dark against a smoke-red sky, and as they hurried on, they left behind them little loosened tufts, tiny strips of cloud which the sunlight steeped in a wine-colored glow.

Mrs. Lyhne sat listening to the wind in the trees. Her head moved very slightly in time with the uneven swelling and sinking of each gust, as it came rushing, swept on boisterously, and died away. But her eyes were far away, farther even than the clouds they gazed on. Pale in her black widow's garb, she sat there with a piteous expression of unrest about her faintly colored lips, while her hands fidgeted with the thick little book on her lap. It was Rousseau's *Héloïse*. Other books were piled up around her: Schiller, Staffeldt, Evald, and Novalis, and large portfolios with prints of old churches and ruins and mountain lakes.

Now she heard doors opening and shutting, then steps that seemed to seek someone in the inner rooms, and presently Niels came in. He had been for a long walk by the fjord. His cheeks were ruddy from the fresh air, and the wind was still in his hair.

Outside, the blue-grey colors had prevailed in the sky, and a few heavy drops of rain splashed against the windows.

Niels told of how high the waves came rolling in and how they had washed the seaweed up on the beach, and about what he had seen and whom he had met. As he talked, he gathered up the books, closed the doors to the garden, and fastened the windows. Then he sat down on the low stool at his mother's feet, took her hand in his, and laid his cheek on her knee.

It had grown quite black outside; the rain beat like hail and ran in streams down casements and panes.

"Do you remember," said Niels after a long silence — "do you
remember how often we sat like this in the dusk and went out in search
of adventures, while father was talking to Jens Overseer in his office,
and Duysen was rattling the teacups in the dining room? And when the
lamp was brought in, we both woke up from our strange adventures to
the sheltered comfort around us, yet I can well remember that I always
thought the story did not stop when we did, but went on unfolding
somewhere under the hills on the way to Ringkjöbing."

He did not see his mother's wistful smile, but he felt her hand passing
gently over his hair.

"Do you remember," she said after a while, "how often you promised
me that when you grew up you would sail out in a big ship and bring
me back all the treasures of the world?"

"Do I remember! I was to bring hyacinths, because you loved hyacinths so much, and a palm like the one that died, and pillars of gold
and marble. There were so many pillars in your stories, always. Do you
remember?"

"I have been waiting for that ship — no, sit still, dear, you don't
understand me — it was not for myself, it was the ship of your fortune. . . . I hoped your life would be full and glorious, that you would
travel on shining paths. . . . Fame — everything — No, not that, if you
would only be one of those who fight for the greatest. I don't know how
it is, but I am so tired of commonplace happiness and commonplace
goals. Do you understand me?"

"You wanted me to be a Sunday child, mother dear, one of those who
do not pull in harness with others, but have their own heaven to be
saved in, and their own place of damnation all to themselves, too. — We
wanted to have flowers on board, didn't we? Gorgeous flowers to strew
over a bleak world; but the ship did not come, and they were poor birds,
Niels and his mother, were they not?"

"Have I hurt you, dear? Why, it was nothing but dreams; don't mind
them!"

Niels was silent a long time, for he felt a shyness about what he wanted
to say. "Mother," he said, "we are not so poor as you think. Some day
the ship will come in. — If you would only believe that and believe in
me. . . . Mother — I am a poet — really — through my whole soul. Don't
imagine this is childish dreams or dreams fed by vanity. If you could
feel my grateful pride in what's best in me — my humble joy in saying
this, so little personal, so far from vainglory, you would believe it just
as I want you to believe it. Dearest, dearest! I *shall* be one of those who
fight for the greatest, and I promise you that I shall not fail, that I shall
always be faithful to myself and my gift. Nothing but the best shall be
good enough. No compromise, mother! When I weigh what I have done

and feel that it isn't sterling, or when I hear that it's got a crack or a flaw — into the melting pot it goes! Every single work must be my best! Do you see why I have to promise? It's my gratitude for my riches that drives me to make vows, and you must receive them. Then if I fail, it will be a sin against you, for it's all owing to you that my soul is like a high-vaulted room — your dreams and longings have given me the impulse to growth, and your sympathies and your unsatisfied thirst for beauty have consecrated me to my lifework."

Mrs. Lyhne wept silently. She felt herself growing pale with rapture. Softly she laid both hands on her son's head, but he drew them gently to his lips and kissed them.

"You have made me so happy, Niels! Then my life has not been one long, useless sigh, if I have helped to lead you on as I hoped and dreamed so ardently — good heavens! how often I have dreamed it! — And yet there is so much sadness mixed in my joy, Niels! To think that my fondest wish should be fulfilled, the thing I have longed for so many years. . . . Such things happen only when life is almost done."

"You mustn't talk like that, you mustn't! Why, everything is going on well, and you are getting stronger every day, mother dear, are you not?"

"It is so hard to die," she said under her breath. "Do you know what I was thinking of in those long sleepless nights, when death seemed so terribly near? I thought the bitterest of all was to know that there were so many great and beautiful things out in the world which I should have to leave behind without ever having seen them. I thought of the thousands and thousands of souls they had lifted up and filled with life and joy, while for me they had not existed. It seemed to me that my soul would fly away poverty-stricken on feeble wings, without any golden memories to carry with it as a reflection from the glories of its homeland, because it had only been sitting in the chimney-corner listening to stories about the wonderful world. — Niels, no one can imagine what agony it is to lie imprisoned in a dull, dark sick room and struggle, in your feverish fancies, to call up before you the beauties of lands you have never seen — snowy Alpine peaks above blue-black mountain lakes, and sparkling rivers between vine-clad banks, and long lines of mountains with ruins peeping out of the woods, and then lofty halls with marble gods — and never to get it quite, but always to give up and start over again, because it seems so terribly hard to leave it without having had the slightest part in it. . . . O God, Niels, to long for it with your whole soul, while you feel that you are being slowly carried to the threshold of another world, to stand on the threshold and look back with a long, long gaze, while all the time you are being forced through that door where none of your longings have gone before you. . . . Niels, take me along in your thoughts, dear, when the time comes for you to share in all that glory which I shall never, never see!"

She wept.

Niels tried to comfort her. He laid bold plans for the journey they would take together as soon as she was quite well. He meant to go to the city to consult a doctor, and he was sure the doctor would agree with him that it was the best thing they could do; So-and-so had traveled and had recovered from his illness completely, simply through the change; a change often worked wonders. He began to trace their route in every detail, spoke of how warmly he would wrap her up, what short trips they would take at first, what a delightful journal they would keep, how they would notice even the smallest trifles, how amusing it would be to eat the queerest things in the loveliest spots, and what awful sins against grammar they would commit in the beginning.

He went on in this strain all that evening and on the days that followed, never wearying. She entered into his plan as into a pleasant fancy, but she was plainly convinced that it would never come to pass.

Nevertheless Niels, acting on the doctor's advice, went on making all the necessary preparations for the trip, and she let him do as he pleased, even fix the day of departure — sure that *that* would happen which would bring all his plans to naught. But when, finally, there were only a few days left, and when her youngest brother, who was to manage the farm in their absence, had actually arrived, she grew uncertain, and now it was she who was most eager to be off, for there still lurked in her mind a fear that the obstacle would leap out and stand in their way at the very last moment.

So they set off.

The first day she was still nervous and uneasy with a lingering trace of her fear, and only when the day was happily ended could she begin to grasp the fact that she was actually on her way to all the glory she had longed for so sorely. Then a feverish joy came over her; her every thought and word was colored by extravagant anticipation, and her thoughts circled unceasingly around what the coming days would bring, one after the other.

And it all came to pass, all that she had hoped, but it did not fill her with rapture nor carry her away with the power or the fervor she had expected. She had imagined it all different, and had imagined herself different, too. In dreams and poems everything had been, as it were, beyond the sea; the haze of distance had mysteriously veiled all the restless mass of details and had thrown out the large lines in bold relief, while the silence of distance had lent its spirit of enchantment. It had been easy then to feel the beauty; but now that she was in the midst of it all, when every little feature stood out and spoke boldly with the manifold voices of reality, and beauty was shattered as light in a prism, she could not gather the rays together again, could not put the picture back beyond the sea. Despondently she was obliged to admit to herself that she felt poor, surrounded by riches that she could not make her own.

She yearned to go on and ever on, still hoping to find a spot she might recognize as a bit of the world she had dreamed, that world which, with every step she took to approach it, seemed to extinguish the magic glamour that had suffused it and to lie spread before her disappointed eyes in the commonplace light of everybody's sun and everybody's moon. But she sought in vain, and as the year was already far advanced, they hastened to Clarens, where the doctor had advised them to spend the winter, and where, moreover, a last faintly gleaming hope lured the tired, dream-wrapped soul; for was it not the Clarens of Rousseau, the Paradise of Julie!

There they remained, but it was of no avail that Winter made himself gentle and held his cold breath from touching her; against the fever in her blood he had no healing. And Spring, when he came on his triumphal march through the valley with the miracle of sprouting seeds and the gospel of budding leaves, he too had to pass her by and let her stand withering in the midst of all this exuberant renascence. The strength that welled out to her from light and air and earth and water could not be transformed to strength within her; it could not make her blood drunk with health nor force it to sing exultantly in the great hymn to the omnipotence of Spring. No, she could but wither, for the last dream that had appeared before her in the dimness of her home as a new reddening dawn, the dream of the glories of the distant world, had not been followed by day. Its colors seemed paler the nearer she came, and she felt that they were pale to her because she had longed for colors that life does not hold and for a beauty that earth cannot ripen. But her longing was not quenched; silent and strong it burned in her heart, hotter in its unstilled thirst, hot and consuming. Round about her, Spring celebrated his feast pregnant with beauty. Snowdrops rang it in with their white bells, and crocuses welcomed it joyfully holding up their veined chalices. Hundreds of tiny mountain streams tumbled headlong down into the valley to report that Spring had come, but they were all too late, for when they trickled between green banks, primroses in yellow and violets in blue stood there and nodded: We know it, we know it; we knew it before you! The willows unfurled their yellow banners, and the curly ferns and the velvety moss hung green garlands over the naked walls of the vineyards, while down below dry nettles hid the stones with long borders of brown and green and faint purple. The grass spread its mantle of green far and wide, and no end of pretty flowers sat down upon it: there were hyacinths with blossoms like stars and blossoms like pearls, legions of daisies, gentians, anemones, dandelions, with a hundred others. And high above this bloom on the ground there floated in the air, borne up by the hoary trunks of aged cherry trees, a thousand shining flower islands, where the light foamed against white shores dotted by blue and red butterflies bringing a message from the flower continent below.

Every day brought new flowers, forcing them out of the ground in motley patterns in the gardens by the sea, pouring them out over the branches of the trees down there — paullinias like giant violets and magnolias like huge purple-stained tulips. Along the paths the flowers advanced in blue and white phalanxes. They filled the meadows with yellow swarms, but nowhere was there such a maze of bloom as in the little sheltered valleys up among the hills, where the larch stood with glittering ruby cones amidst pale green needles, for there the narcissus blossomed in dazzling myriads, filling the air far and wide with the drowsy fragrance from their white orgies.

With all this beauty round about her, she still sat there with the old unanswered longing for beauty in her heart. It was only now and then, when the sun sank behind the gentle slopes of Savoy, and the mountains beyond the sea seemed made of brown opaque glass, as if their precipitous sides had drunk the light, that nature could hold her senses spellbound. Then, when the bright yellow mists of evening veiled the distant Jura Mountains, and the lake, like a copper mirror from which tongues of golden flame shot into the red sunset glow, seemed to melt with the sky into one vast, shining infinity — then it would seem, once in a great while, as though the longing were silenced, and the soul had found the land it sought.

As spring advanced, her strength failed more and more. Soon she did not leave her bed, but she was no longer afraid of death; she awaited it eagerly, for she cherished the hope that beyond the grave she would be face to face with all the glory, be one in soul with the fullness of beauty which here on earth had drawn her in hope and yearning — a yearning which had been clarified and transfigured by the increasing pain of long empty years and thus prepared to attain its goal. She dreamed many a gentle, wistful dream of how she would return in memory to what earth had given her, return from the land of immortality, where all the beauty of the earth would be always beyond the sea.

So she died, and Niels buried her in the friendly churchyard at Clarens, where the brown vineyard mold covers the children of so many lands, and where broken columns and veiled urns repeat the same words of mourning in so many languages.

They gleam white under dark cypresses and among the winter bloom of the viburnum; early roses strew their petals over many of them, and often the ground at their base is blue with violets, but over every mound and every stone creep the glossy-leaved vines of the gentle periwinkle, Rousseau's favorite flower, sky blue as never a sky was blue.

Chapter IX

*N*iels Lyhne hurried home. He could not bear his loneliness among so many strangers, but the nearer he came to Copenhagen, the oftener he asked himself what he wanted there, and the more he regretted that he had not stayed abroad. For whom did he have in Copenhagen? Not Frithjof, and Erik was traveling in Italy on a scholarship, so he was not there. Mrs. Boye? It was a queer affair, this relation with Mrs. Boye. Now that he came straight from his mother's grave, it seemed to him, not exactly a desecration or anything like that, and yet out of tune with the key in which his present moods were pitched. It was discord. If he had been going to meet his fiancée, his young blushing bride, now that his soul had so long been bent on filial duties, it would not have conflicted with his feeling. It was of no use that he tried to take a superior tone with himself and call the change in his conception of his intimacy with Mrs. Boye Philistine and provincial. The word "Bohemian" formed itself subconsciously as an expression of a distaste that he could not reason away, and it was in line with this mood that his first visit, after he had engaged his old rooms at the embankment, was to the Neergaards and not to Mrs. Boye.

The following day he called on her, but did not find her in. The janitor said she had taken a villa at Emilie-kilde, which surprised Niels, for he knew that her father's country house was in that neighborhood.

Well, he would have to go out there in a day or two.

But the very next day he received a note from Mrs. Boye asking him to meet her in her apartment in town. The pale niece had seen him in the street. A quarter before one he was to come — he *must* come. She would tell him why, *if he did not know it.* Did he know it? He must not misjudge her, and not be unreasonable. He knew her too well, and why should he take it as a plebeian nature would? He must not — please! After all, they were not like other people. Oh, if he only *would* understand her! Niels, Niels!

This letter made him strangely excited, and he suddenly remembered with a sense of uneasiness that Mrs. Neergaard had looked at him with a sarcastic pitying expression and had smiled and said nothing in a curious meaning way. What could it be? What in the world could have happened?

The mood that had kept him away from Mrs. Boye had vanished so completely that he could not understand how he had ever felt it. He was alarmed. If they had only written to each other like sensible people! *Why* had they not written? He certainly had not been so busy. It was queer how he would allow himself to be so absorbed in the place where he happened to be that he forgot what was far away, or if he did not forget it, at least pushed it into the distant background, where it was buried by the present — as under mountains. No one would think he had imagination.

At last! Mrs. Boye herself opened the door to the anteroom before he had time to ring. She said nothing, but gave him her hand in a long, sympathetic clasp; the newspapers had announced his bereavement. Niels said nothing either, and so they walked silently through the parlor, between the two rows of chairs in red-striped covers. The chandelier was wrapped in paper, and the windowpanes were whitened. In the sitting room everything was as usual, except that the Venetian blinds were rolled down before the opened windows, and as they moved to and fro in the slight breeze, they struck the casement with a faint, monotonous tapping. Rays of light reflected from the sunlit canal outside filtered in between the yellow slats and made squares of tremulous wavy lines in the ceiling, which quivered with the rippling of the wave outside. Otherwise all was hushed and still, silently waiting with bated breath....

Mrs. Boye could not make up her mind where she wanted to sit; finally she decided on the rocking chair, and dusted it assiduously with her handkerchief, but instead of sitting down she stood behind the chair, resting her hands on its back. She still wore her gloves and had only drawn one arm out of her half-fitting black mantilla. Her dress was of silk tartan in a very tiny check matching the broad ribbons on the wide, round Pamela hat of light straw which half hid her face as she stood looking down and rocking the chair nervously.

Niels seated himself on the piano stool at a distance from her, as if he expected something unpleasant.

"Then you know it, Niels?"

"No, but what is it I don't know?"

The chair stopped. "I am engaged."

"Are you engaged? But how — why — Mrs. Boye?"

"Oh, don't call me Mrs. Boye, and don't begin to be unreasonable right away!" She leaned against the back of the rocking chair with a little air of defiance. "Surely you can understand that it isn't the pleasantest thing in the world for me to stand here and explain to you. I will do it, but you might at least help me."

"What do you mean? Are you engaged, or are you not?"

"I have just told you that I am," she replied with gentle impatience, looking up.

"Then may I be allowed to wish you joy, Mrs. Boye, and to thank you very much for the time we have known each other." He had risen to his feet and bowed sarcastically several times.

"And you can part from me like this, quite calmly? I am engaged, and then we are done, and everything that has been between us two is just a stupid old story which mustn't be brought to mind anymore. Past is past, and that is all — Niels, all the precious days — will the memory of them be silent from now on? Will you never, never think of me, never miss me? Won't you call the dream forth again, on many a quiet evening, and give it the colors it might have glowed with? Can you keep from loving it all back to life again in your thoughts and ripening it to the fullness it might have had? Can you? Can you put your foot on it and crush it all out of existence, every bit of it? Niels!"

"I hope so; you have shown me that it can be done. — But this is nonsense, pure, unmitigated nonsense from the beginning to end. Why did you arrange this comedy? I have no shadow of a right to reproach you. You have never loved, never said that you loved me. You have given me leave to love you, that is all, and now you withdraw your permission. Or perhaps you will allow me to go on, though you have given yourself to another? I don't understand you, if you can imagine that to be possible. We are not children. Or are you afraid I shall forget you too soon? Never fear. You are not one to be blotted easily out of a man's life. But take care! A love like mine does not come to a woman twice in her life; take care that you do not bring misfortune upon yourself by casting me off! I don't wish you any harm, no, no! May you never know want and sickness, and may you have all the happiness that comes with wealth, admiration, and social success, in measure full and overflowing, that is my wish for you. May all the world stand open to you, all but one little door, one single little door, however much you knock and try to open it — but otherwise everything as fully and widely as it is possible to wish it."

He spoke slowly, almost sadly, not bitterly, but with a strangely tremulous note in his voice, a note that was new to her and moved her. She had grown a little pale and stood leaning stiffly against the chair. "Niels," she said, "don't predict misfortune! Remember you were not here. Niels, and my love — I did not know now real it was; it seemed more like something that just interested me. It breathed through my life like a delicate spiritual poem, it never caught me in strong arms; it had wings — only wings. At least I thought so, I did not know better until now, or until the moment I had done it — said Yes and all that. Everything was so difficult, there were so many things all at once and so many people to consider. . . . It began with my brother, Hardenskjold, the one who was in the West Indies, you know. He had been rather wild when he was here, but over there he settled down and became so sensible and went into partnership with someone and made a lot of money, and married a rich widow, a sweet little thing, I assure you, and he and father made up, for Hardie was so changed, oh, he is so respectable there is no end to it, and so susceptible to what people say — terribly bourgeois, oh! Of course, he thought I ought to be taken up in the bosom of the family again, and every time he came here he lectured me and pleaded and palavered, and you see, father is an old man now, and so at last I did it, and everything was just as in the old days."

She paused for a moment and began to take off first her mantilla and then her hat and gloves, and, busy with all this, she turned a little away from Niels, while she went on talking.

"And then Hardie had a friend who is very highly respected — oh, extremely so, and they all thought I ought to do it and wished it so much, and then you see I could take my position in society just as before, or really better than before, because he is so very highly respected in every way, and after all that is what I have been wishing for a long time. I suppose you can't understand that? You would never have thought it of me? Quite the contrary. Because I was always making fun of conventional society with its banalities and its stereotyped morality, its thermometer of virtue and its compass of womanliness — you remember how witty we were! It is to weep, Niels, for it wasn't true, at least not all the time. I will tell you something: we women can break away for a while, when something in our lives has opened our eyes to the love of freedom that after all is in us, but we can't keep it up. It is in our blood, this passion for the quintessence of propriety and the pinnacle of gentility up to its most punctilious point. We can't bear to be at war with the established order that is accepted by all commonplace people. In our inmost selves we really think these people are right, because they are the ones that sit in judgment, and in our hearts we bow to their judgments and suffer from them, no matter how brave a face we wear.

It is not natural for us women to be exceptional, not really, Niels, it makes us so queer, more interesting, perhaps, but still — Can you understand it? It is silly, don't you think so? But at least you can comprehend that it made a strange impression on me to return to the old surroundings. So many things came back to me, memories of my mother and of her standards. It seemed as though I had come into a safe haven again; everything was so peaceful and well ordered, and I had only to bind myself to it to be properly happy ever after. And so I let them bind me, Niels."

Niels could not help smiling; he felt so superior, and was so sorry for her, as she stood there, girlishly unhappy in the midst of all this confession. He was softened and could not find any hard words.

He went over to her.

Meanwhile she had turned the chair toward her and had sunk down on it, and now she was sitting there quite forlorn and pathetic, leaning back with arms hanging and face lifted, gazing out under lowered eyelids through the darkened parlor with its two rows of chairs into the dim anteroom.

Niels laid his arm along the back of the chair and rested his hand on its arm, as he bent over her. "And you had quite forgotten — me?" he whispered.

She seemed not to hear him and did not even lift her eyes, but at last she shook her head, very faintly, and, after another long pause, shook it again, very faintly.

Round about them everything was very still at first. Then a maid came clattering along the halls and singing, as she polished the door locks; the noise of the knobs turning cut brutally into the silence and made it seem deeper than before when it suddenly came back. After a while, nothing was heard except the drowsy, monotonous tapping of the blinds.

The silence seemed to rob them of the power of speech, almost of thought. She sat as before with her eyes fixed on the dim anteroom, while he remained standing, bending over her, gazing at the pattern of her silk dress, and, unconsciously, lured by the enveloping stillness, he began to rock her in the chair — very — softly — very — softly. . . .

She lifted her eyelids for a look at his shadowed profile, and lowered them again in quiet content. It was like a long embrace; it was as though she gave herself into his arms when the chair went back, and when it swung forward again, and her feet touched the floor, there was something of him in the pressure of the boards against her foot. He felt it too; the process began to interest him, and he rocked more and more vigorously. It was as though he came nearer and nearer to taking her as he drew the chair farther back; there was anticipation in the instant when it was about to plunge forward again, and when it came down there was a strange satisfaction in the soft tap of her passive feet against the floor; then when he pushed it down yet a little farther there was complete possession in the action which pressed her sole gently against the floor and forced her to raise her knee ever so slightly.

"Let us not dream!" said Niels at last with a sigh and relinquished the chair.

"Yes, let us!" she said almost pleadingly, and looked innocently at him with great wistful eyes.

She had risen slowly.

"No dreams!" said Niels nervously, putting his arm around her waist. "Too many dreams have passed between you and me. Have you never felt them? Have they never touched you like a light breath caressing your cheek or stirring your hair? Is it possible that the night has never been tremulous with sigh upon sigh that dropped and died on your lips?"

He kissed her, and it seemed to him that she grew less young under his kisses, less young, but lovelier, more glowing in her beauty, more alluring.

"I want you to know it," he said. "You don't know how I love you, how I have suffered and longed. Oh, if those rooms at the embankment could speak, Tema!"

He kissed her again and again, and she threw her arms around his neck with such abandon that her wild silk sleeves fell back above the billowing lace of the white undersleeves, above the grey elastic that held them together over the elbow.

"What could those rooms say, Niels?"

"Tema, they could say, ten thousand times and more; they could pray in that name, rage in that name, sigh and sob in it; they could threaten Tema, too."

"Could they?"

From the street below came a conversation floating in through the open window complete and unabridged, the most commonplace worldly wisdom drawled in shopworn phrases, welded together by two untemperamental, gossipy voices. All this prose made it more wonderful yet to stand there, heart to heart, sheltered in the soft, dim light.

"How I love you, sweetheart, sweetheart — in my arms you are so dear! are you so dear, so dear? And your hair — I can hardly speak, and all my memories — so dear-all my memories of how I cried and was wretched and longed so miserably, they press on and force their way in as if they too would be happy with me in my happiness — do you understand? — Do you remember, Tema, the moonlight last year? Are you fond of it? — Oh, you don't know how cruel it can be. Such a clear moonlight night, when the air seems to have stiffened in cold light, and the clouds lie there in long layers — Tema, flowers and leaves hold their fragrance so close around them it is like a frost of scents covering them, and all sounds seem so far away and die so suddenly and do not linger at all — Such a night is so merciless, for it makes longing grow so strangely intense; the silence draws it out from every corner of your soul, sucks it out with hard lips, and there is no glimmering hope, no slumbering promise in all that clearness. Oh, how I cried, Tema! Tema, have you never cried through a moonlight night? Sweetheart, it would be a shame if you should cry; you shall never cry, there shall always be sunshine for you and nights of roses — a night of roses —"

She had given herself entirely to his embrace, and with her gaze lost in his, her lips murmured strangely sweet words of love, half muted by her breath, words repeated after him, as if she were whispering them to her own heart.

The cessation of the voices in the street made her stir restlessly. Then they came back to the firm, rhythmic accompaniment of a cane striking against the cobblestones, crossed over to the other side, lingered long in the distance, sank to a murmur — died away.

And the silence again welled up around them, flamed up around them, throbbing with heartbeats, heavy with breath, yielding. Speech had been seared away between them, and lingering kisses fell from their lips fraught with unspoken questions, but giving no solace nor any present bliss. They held each other's gaze and dared not take their eyes away, but neither did they dare to put meaning into their look; they veiled it rather; withdrew behind it, silently hiding, brooding over secret dreams.

A quiver passed through his clasping arms and woke her. She thrust him from her with both hands and set herself free.

"Go, Niels, go! You must not be here, you must not. Do you hear?"

He tried to draw her to him again, but she broke away, wild and pale. She was trembling from head to foot and stood holding her arms out from her body as if she were afraid to touch herself.

Niels would have knelt and caught her hand.

"Don't touch me!" There was desperation in her look. "Why don't you go when I am begging you to? Good heavens, why can't you go? No, no, don't speak to me, go away, you — Can't you see I am shaking before you? Look! Oh, it's wicked the way you are treating me! And when I am begging you to go!"

It was impossible to say a word; she would not listen. She was quite beside herself. Tears streamed from her eyes; her face was almost distorted and seemed to give out light in its pallor.

"Oh, do go! Can't you see that you are humiliating me by staying? You are brutal to me, that's what you are! What have I done to you that you ill-treat me this way? Do go! Have you no pity?"

Pity? He was cold with rage. This was madness! Still he could do nothing but go, and he went. He did not like the two rows of chairs, but he walked slowly between them, looking at them with a fixed gaze of defiance.

"Exit Niels Lyhne," he said, when he heard the latch of the hall-door click behind him.

He walked down the steps thoughtfully, his hat in his hand. On the landing he stopped and gesticulated to himself: If he could understand the least bit! Why *this* and why, again, *that?* Then he walked on. There were the open windows. He felt like tearing to pieces that sickly sweet silence up there with a shrill cry. He felt like talking to someone for hours — mercilessly-talking nonsense into that silence, washing it cold in nonsense. He could not get it out of his blood; he could see it, taste it; he walked in it. Suddenly he stopped and blushed fiery red with angry shame. Had she used him to tempt herself with?

In the room above, Mrs. Boye still was weeping. She had gone over to the pier glass and stood resting both hands on the console, weeping till the tears dripped from her cheeks down into the pink chamber of a huge sea shell lying there. She looked at her distorted face as it appeared above the misty spot her breath had formed on the mirror, and traced the course of her tears as they welled out over the rim of the eyes and rolled down. Where did they all come from? She had never cried like this before — yes, once, in Frascati, after a runaway.

Presently the tears began to come more sparingly, but a nervous trembling still shook her spasmodically from neck to heel.

The sun now beat directly on the windows. The tremulous reflections from the waves were drawn aslant under the ceiling, and on the sides of the Venetian blinds the parallel rays fell in rows, forming perfect shelves of yellow light. The heat increased, and mingling with the ripe smell of hot wood and sun-warmed dust, other scents floated out from the bright flowers of the sofa cushions, from the silken curves of the chair backs, from books and folded rugs, where the heat released *a* hundred forgotten perfumes and wafted them through the air, light as wraiths.

Very slowly her trembling subsided, leaving a curious dizziness, in which fantastic emotions that were more than half sensations whirled around on the track of her wondering thoughts. She closed her eyes, but remained standing with her face turned to the mirror.

Strange how it had come over her, this piercing terror! Had she cried out? There was the echo of a scream in her ears and a tired feeling in her throat as if she had emitted a long, anguished cry. If he had taken her! She allowed herself to be taken and pressed her arms against her heart as if to ward him off. She struggled, but yet — now: she felt as if she were sinking with shame, impudently caressed by all the winds of heaven — He would not go, and it would soon be too late; all her strength was leaving her like bubbles that burst; bubble after bubble forced its way between her lips and burst unceasingly; in another second it would be too late! Had she begged him on her knees? Too late! She was lifted irresistibly to his embrace, as a bubble that rises through the water — tremulous, so her soul rose up naked before him, with every wish bared to his gaze, every secret dream, hidden surrender unveiled before his mastering eye. Again in his arms, lingering, sweetly trembling. There was a statue of alabaster surrounded by flames; it glowed transparent in the heat of the fire; little by little its dark center melted, until all was luminous light.

Slowly she opened her eyes and looked at her image in the mirror with a discreet smile as at a fellow conspirator before whom she did not wish to commit herself too fully. Then she went around the room gathering together her gloves, hat, and mantilla.

Her dizziness seemed blown away, leaving only a rather pleasant sense of weakness in her knees. She walked about to feel it better. Secretly, as if by accident, she gave the rocking chair a confidential little push with her elbow.

She rather liked scenes.

With one look she said farewell to some invisible thing. Then she rolled up the blinds, and it seemed like another room.

*T*hree weeks later Mrs. Boye was married, and Niels Lyhne was quite alone with himself. He could not quite keep up his indignation over the unworthy manner in which she had thrown herself into the arms of that conventional society at which she had so often scoffed. True, it had only opened the door and beckoned, and she had come. But it was hardly for him to throw stones, for had he not himself felt the magnetic attraction of honest bourgeoisie? If it had not been for that last meeting! If that really was what he accused her of, if it had been intended for a madcap farewell to the old life, one last wanton prank before she withdrew behind "the quintessence of propriety" — could it be possible? Such boundless self-scorn, such a cynical mockery of herself and him and all that they had shared of memories and hopes, of enthusiasm and sacred ideals! It made him blush and rage by turns. — But was he fair to her? After all, what had she done but tell him frankly and honestly: Such and such things draw me to the other side and draw me powerfully, but I recognize your right even more fully than you ask, and here I am. If you can take me, I am yours; if not, I go where the power is greatest. — And if it were so, had she not been entirely within her rights? He had not been able to take her. The final decision *might* depend on such a little thing, on the shadow of a thought, the vibration of a mood.

If he only knew what she must have known for an instant and probably did not know any longer! He hated to believe that of which he could not help accusing her. Not only for her sake, but even more for his own, because it seemed to put a blot on his 'scutcheon, not logically, of course, and yet-But, whatever the manner of her leaving him, one thing was certain: he was now alone, and though he felt the emptiness at first, he was soon conscious of a sense of relief. So many things were waiting for him. The year at Lönborggaard and abroad, though absorbing his thoughts, had been in a sense an involuntary rest, and the very fact that this period had given him a clearer conception of his own powers and limitations spurred him on to use his faculties in undisturbed work. He was not anxious to create yet, but rather to collect; there was such an infinite mass of material he wanted to make his own that he began to think dejectedly of the brief span of mortal life. Though he had never wasted his time, it is not easy to emancipate one's self from the paternal bookcase, and it seems simplest to seek the goal along the paths where others have attained it, and therefore he had not set out to seek his own Vinland in the wide world of books, but had followed where the fathers led. Loyally he had closed his eyes to much that lured him, in order to see more clearly in the vast night of the Eddas and sagas, and he had been deaf to many voices that called him, in order to listen more closely to the mystic sounds of nature in the folk songs.

But now he understood, at last, that it was not a law of nature to be either Old Norse or Romantic, that it was simpler to express his own doubts than to put them in the mouth of Gorm, Loki-worshipper, that it was more rational to find words for the mystic stirrings of his own being than to call to the cloister walls of the Middle Ages and hear his own voice come back to him as a faint echo.

He had always had an open mind for the new ideas of his time, but he had been occupied in finding how the New had been foreshadowed in the Old, rather than in listening to what the New said clearly and explicitly for itself. In this he was in no wise remarkable; for never yet has any new gospel been preached but the whole world has become busy with the old prophets.

Yet this did not suffice, and Niels threw himself enthusiastically into his new labors. He was seized with that lust of conquest and thirst for the power of knowledge which every worker in the realm of thought, no matter how humble a drvidge he may later become, has surely felt once in his life, though for only one brief hour. Which one of us all, whom a kind fate has given the opportunity to care for the development of our own minds, has not gazed rapturously out over the boundless sea of knowledge, and which of us has not gone down to its clear, cool waters and begun, in the light-hearted arrogance of youth, to dip it out in our hollow hand as the child in the legend? Do you remember how the sun could laugh over the fair summer land, yet you saw neither flower nor sky nor rippling brook? The feasts of life swept past and woke not even a dream in your young blood; even your home seemed far away — do you remember? And do you also remember how a structure rose in your thoughts from the yellowing leaves of books, complete and whole, reposing in itself as a work of art, and it was yours in every detail, and your spirit dwelt in it? When the pillars rose slender and with conscious strength in their bold curves, it was of you that brave aspiring and of you the bold sustaining. And when the vaulted roof seemed to be suspended in air, because it had gathered all its weight, stone upon stone, in mighty drops, and let it down on the neck of the pillars, it was of you that dream of weightless floating, that confident bearing down of the arches; it was you planting your foot on your own.

In this wise your personality grows with your knowledge and is clarified and unified through it. To learn is as beautiful as to live. Do not be afraid to lose yourself in minds greater than your own! Do not sit brooding anxiously over your own individuality or shut yourself out from influences that draw you powerfully for fear that they may sweep you along and submerge your innermost pet peculiarities in their mighty surge! Never fear! The individuality that can be lost in the sifting and reshaping of a healthy development is only a flaw; it is a branch grown in the dark, which is distinctive only so long as it retains its sickly pallor. And it is by the sound growth in yourself that you must live. Only the sound can grow great.

Christmas Eve came upon Niels Lyhne unawares. For the past six months, he had not visited anyone except now and then the Neergaards. They had invited him to spend the evening with them, but last Christmas Eve had been the memorable one at Clarens, and therefore he preferred to be alone.

There was a high wind. A thin covering of snow not yet trodden into slush spread over the streets and made them seem wider. The layer of white on roofs and windowsills gave a touch of beauty to the houses at the same time as it made them appear more isolated. The street lamps, flickering in the wind, would now and then, as if absent-mindedly, send a patch of light up a wall and startle from its dreams a merchant's sign, making it stare out in large-lettered blankness. The store windows, too, half lighted as they were and still disarranged from the Christmas shopping, wore an unusual aspect, a curiously abstracted look.

He turned into the side streets, where the celebration seemed to be in full swing. Music sounded from basements and low rooms; sometimes it was a violin, but more often a hand organ, that droned out dance tunes, and sometimes in the hearty goodwill of the performers suggested rather the pleasant toil of the dance than its festive glamour. It brought an illusion of shuffling feet and steaming air — at least so it seemed to him who stood outside and, in his solitude, became polemical against all this sociability. He had much more sympathy for the workingman who stood with his child outside a tiny shop, discussing one of the cheap marvels in the dimly lighted window, evidently determined to have their choice absolutely decided before they ventured into that den of temptation. And he felt sympathy for the poorly clad old gentlewomen who passed him, one by one, almost at every hundred steps — all with the strangest coats and mantillas in the fashion of bygone days, and all with diffident, timorous movements of their old throats, like suspicious birds, walking in the uncertain, hesitating manner of those long unused to the world, as if they had been sitting, day after day, forgotten in the hidden corners of rear flats and attic rooms and only that one evening in the year were included and remembered. It saddened him. His heart shrank with a sick sensation, as he tried to picture to himself the slowly trickling existence of such a lonely old spinster; he seemed to hear sounding in his ears a mantel clock, painfully rhythmic, ticking out its "once-again, once-again," dropping the empty seconds, one by one in the chalice of day and filling it full.

Well, he would have to get this Christmas dinner over with. He retraced his steps in a half conscious dread that if he chose other streets they might reveal other kinds of lonely creatures and other forms of forlornness than those he had encountered, which had already left a bitter taste in his mouth.

Out there in the wider streets he breathed more freely. He quickened his pace with a slight sense of defiance, holding himself apart as it were from what he had just seen by telling himself that his loneliness was self-chosen.

He entered one of the larger restaurants. While waiting for his dinner, he observed, from the shelter of an old newspaper supplement, the people who came in. Most of them were young men. Some had a challenging air, as if they would forbid all present to appropriate them as fellow sufferers, while others could not conceal their embarrassment at having no place to go on such an evening, but all showed a marked preference for distant corners and secluded tables. Many came in couples, and most of these were plainly brothers; Niels had never seen so many brothers all at once. Often they were very much unlike each other in dress and manner, and their hands testified even more clearly to their different positions in life. It was almost a rarity to see any particular intimacy between them, either when they came or after they had sat and talked for a while. Here, one was superior and the other full of admiration; there, one was cordial, while the other repelled advances. Others again betrayed a mutual watchfulness, or, worse yet, an unexpressed condemnation of each other's aims and ambitions and methods. Most of them evidently needed the holiday and a certain amount of loneliness to make them remember their common origin and bring them together.

Niels sat thinking of this and marveling at the patience all these people exhibited, neither ringing nor calling for the waiters, as if they had tacitly agreed to banish as much as possible of the restaurant atmosphere from the place. While he was engrossed in this, he saw just coming in a man whom he knew, and the sudden sight of a familiar face among all these strangers startled him so that he rose and met him with a pleased, though somewhat surprised, "Good evening."

"Are you waiting for anyone?" asked the other, looking for a place to hang his overcoat. "No, I am alone."

"That's lucky for me!"

The newcomer was a Dr. Hjerrild, a young man whom Niels had met at the Neergaards, and whom he knew — not from anything he had said, but from certain innuendos of Mrs. Neergaard's — to be very liberal in his religious views, though the political opinions he professed were quite the reverse. People of that type did not often frequent the home of the Neergaards, who were at once religious and liberal. The doctor, however, belonged by inclination as well as through the influence of his dead mother to one of the circles — rather numerous at that time — where the new liberal ideas were looked on with skeptical or even hostile eyes, while in religion their members were rather more than rationalists and rather less than atheists, when they were not mystics or indifferentists. These various circles had many shades of opinion, but, in general, they were agreed in feeling that Holstein was at least as near to their hearts as Slesvig, while the kinship with Sweden was ignored, and Danism in its newest forms was not altogether approved. Moreover, they knew their Molière better than their Holberg, Baggesen better than Oehlenschlager, and in their artistic taste they tended, perhaps, to the sentimental.

In such, or at least kindred influences, Hjerrild had developed. He sat looking a little dubiously at Niels, as the latter recounted his observations of the other diners and especially dwelt on their apparent shame at not having part in any home or semblance of home on such an evening.

"I understand that perfectly," he said coldly, in a tone almost of rebuff. "People don't come here on Christmas Eve because they like it, and necessarily they must have a sense of humiliation at being left out, no matter whether it's other people's doing or their own. Do you mind telling me why you are here? Don't answer if you would rather not."

Niels replied that it was only because he had spent last Christmas Eve with his mother, who had since died.

"I beg your pardon," said Hjerrild; "it was very good of you to answer me, and you must forgive me for being so suspicious. Do you know, I could very well imagine that you might come here in order to administer a youthful kick to Christmas as an institution, but as for myself, I am really here out of respect for other people's Christmas. It is the first Christmas Eve since I came here that I have not spent with a very kind family from my native town. It occurred to me, somehow, that I was in the way when they sang their Christmas carols, not that they were ashamed — they have too much character for that — but it made them uneasy to have anyone there to whom these hymns were as sung into the empty air. At least that is what I imagined."

Almost silently they finished their dinner, lighted their cigars, and agreed to go somewhere else for their toddy. Neither of them felt inclined, that evening, to gaze upon the same gilded mirror frames and red sofas that met their eyes on most of the other evenings of the year, and so they sought refuge in a little café which they did not usually frequent.

They soon realized that this was no place to stay in.

The host and the waiters, with a few friends, sat in the rear of the room, playing loo with two trumps. The host's wife and daughters looked on and brought the refreshments, but not to the strangers; a waiter filled their order. They drank hurriedly, for they noticed that their entrance made an interruption; the conversation was hushed, and the host, who had been sitting in his shirt sleeves, seemed embarrassed and put on his coat.

"We seem to be rather homeless tonight," said Niels, as they walked down the street.

"Well, that is as it should be," was Hjerrild's rather pathetic answer.

They began to talk about the Christian religion, for the topic was in the air.

Niels argued vehemently, but in rather general terms, against Christianity.

Hjerrild was tired of treading again the beaten track of discussions that were old to him, and suddenly said, without any particular connection with what had gone before: "Take care, Lyhne; Christianity is in power. It is foolish to quarrel with the reigning truth by agitating for a crown prince truth."

"Foolish or not foolish — what does it matter?"

"Don't say that so lightly. I did not mean to tell you such a commonplace as that it is foolish in a material way; morally, too, it is foolish and worse. Take care, don't associate yourself too closely with this particular movement in our time, unless it happens to be absolutely necessary to your own personality. As a poet you must have many other interests."

"I don't understand you. I can't treat myself like a hurdy-gurdy from which I can take out an unpopular piece and put in a tune that everybody is whistling."

"Can't you? Many people can. But you can at least say: 'We are not playing that piece just now.' We can often do more in that line than we think. A human being is not so closely knit. When you use your right arm constantly in violent exertion, the blood rushes to it, and it grows at the expense of the rest of your body, while your legs, which you are using as little as possible, naturally get a little thin. You can apply the image for yourself. Have you noticed that most of the idealistic forces in our country, and probably the best of them, are entirely absorbed in the cause of political freedom? You can take a lesson from that. Believe me, there is saving grace in fighting for an idea that is gaining ground, but it is very demoralizing to a man to belong to a losing minority, which life, in its inevitable course, puts in the wrong, point by point, step by step. It cannot be otherwise, for it is bitterly disheartening to see that which your inmost soul believes to be right and true, to see this Truth reviled and struck in the face by the meanest camp follower in the victorious army, to hear her called vile names, while you can do nothing at all except to love her even more faithfully, kneel to her in your heart with even deeper adoration, and see her beautiful face as radiantly beautiful as ever and as full of majesty, shining with the same immortal light, no matter how much dust is whirled up around her white forehead, no matter how thickly the poisonous fog closes around her halo. It is bitterly disheartening, and your soul suffers injury inevitably, for it is so easy to hate until you heart is weary, or to draw around you the cold shadows of contempt, or to be dulled by pain and let the world go its own way. — Of course, if there is *that* within you which makes you not choose the easiest way nor evade the whole matter, but walk upright with all your faculties tense and all your sympathies wide awake, taking the blows and stings of defeat as the scourge falls on your back again and again, and still keep your bleeding hope from dropping, while you listen for the distant rumblings that presage revolution, and look for the faint, distant dawn that some day — some time, perhaps . . . If you have *that* within you! — but don't try it, Lyhne. Imagine what the life of such a man must be, if he is to be true to himself. Never to open his mouth without knowing that whatever he says will be met with scorn and jeers! To have his words distorted, besmirched, wrenched all out of joint, turned into cunning snares for his own feet, and then, before he can pick them up from the mud and straighten them out again, to find all the world suddenly deaf. Then to begin over again at another point and have the same thing happen over and over again. And — what hurts most, perhaps — to be misunderstood and despised by noble men and women, whom he looks up to with admiration and respect in spite of their different principles. Yet it must be so, it cannot be otherwise. Those who are in opposition must not expect to be attacked for what they really are or really want, but for what the party in power is pleased to think they are and want; and besides, power used upon the weaker must be misused — how can it be otherwise? Surely no one can expect the party in power to divest itself of its advantages in order to meet the opposition on equal terms; but that does not make the struggle of the opposition less painful and heart-rending. When you think of all this, Lyhne, do you really suppose a man can fight this battle, with all these vulture beaks buried in his flesh, unless he has the blind stubborn enthusiasm which we call fanaticism? And how in the world can he get fanatic about a negation? Fanatic for the idea that there is no God! — But without fanaticism there is no victory. Hush, listen!"

They stopped before a house where a curtain had been rolled up, allowing them to look into a large room, and through the slightly opened window a song floated out to them, borne on the clear voices of women and children:

"A child is born in Bethlehem,
   In Bethlehem.
Therefore rejoice, Jerusalem!
   Hallelujah, Hallelujah!"

They walked on silently. The song and especially the notes of the piano followed them down the quiet street.

"Did you hear?" said Hjerrild. "Did you hear the enthusiasm in that old Hebraic shout of triumph? And those two Jewish names of towns! Jerusalem was not only symbolic: the entire city, Copenhagen, Denmark, it was *Us*, the Christian people within the people."

"There is no God, and man is his prophet," replied Niels bitterly and rather sadly.

"Exactly," scoffed Hjerrild. "After all, atheism is unspeakably tame. Its end and aim is nothing but a disillusioned humanity. The belief in a God who rules everything and judges everything is humanity's last great illusion, and when that is gone, what then? Then you are wiser; but richer, happier? I can't see it."

"But don't you see," exclaimed Niels Lyhne, "that on the day when men are free to exult and say: 'There is no God!' on that day a new heaven and a new earth will be created as if by magic. Then and not till then will heaven be a free infinite space instead of a spying, threatening eye. Then the earth will be ours and we the earth's, when the dim world of bliss or damnation beyond has burst like a bubble. The earth will be our true mother country, the home of our hearts, where we dwell, not as strangers and wayfarers a short time, but all our time. Think what intensity it will give to life, when everything must be concentrated within it and nothing left for a hereafter. The immense stream of love that is now rising up to the God of men's faith will bend to earth again and flow lovingly among all those beautiful human virtues with which we have endowed and embellished the godhead in order to make it worthy of our love. Goodness, justice, wisdom — who can name them all? Don't you see what nobility it will give men when they are free to live their life and die their death, without fear of hell or hope of heaven, but fearing themselves, hoping for themselves? How their consciences will grow, and what a strength it will give them when inactive repentance and humility cannot atone anymore, when no forgiveness is possible except to redeem with good what they sinned with evil."

"You must have a wonderful faith in humanity. Why, then atheism will make greater demands on men than Christianity has done."

"Of course!"

"Of course; but where will you get all the strong individuals you will need to make up your atheistical community?"

"Little by little; atheism itself must develop them. Neither this generation nor the next and not the next after that will be ripe for atheism, of that I am quite aware, but in every generation there will be a few who will honestly struggle to live and die in it and will win. These people will, in course of time, form a group of spiritual ancestors to whom their descendants will look back in pride, and from whom they will gain courage. It will be hardest in the beginning; many will fail, and those who win will have torn banners, because they will still be steeped in traditions to the marrow of their bones; it is not only the brain that has to be convinced, but the blood and nerves, hopes and longings, even dreams! But it does not matter; some time it will come, and the few will be the many."

"You think so? — I am trying to think of a name; could we call it pietistical atheism?"

"All true atheism —" Niels began, but Hjerrild cut him short.

"Of course," he said, "of course! By all means, let us have only a single gate, one needle's eye for all the camels on the face of the earth."

Chapter X

*E*arly that summer Erik Refstrap came home after his two years in Italy. He had gone away a sculptor; he returned a painter, and he had already attracted attention, had sold his pictures, and received orders for others.

The good fortune coming almost at his first call was due to the sure instinct for self-limitation which bound his art closely to his own personality. His gift was not of the large and generous kind that is instinct with every promise and seems about to grasp every laurel, that sweeps triumphantly through every realm like a bacchanalian troop, scattering golden seed on every side, and mounting genii on all its panthers! He was one of those in whom a dream is buried, making a peaceful sanctuary in one corner of their souls where they are most, and yet least, themselves. Through everything these people create there sounds the same wistful refrain, and every work of art that comes from their hands bears the same timidly circumscribed stamp of kinship, as if they were all pictures from the same little homeland, the same little nook deep among mountains. It was so with Erik; no matter where he plunged into the ocean of beauty, he always fetched the same pearl up to the light.

His canvases were small: in the foreground a single figure, clay blue with its own shadow, behind it a heathery stretch of moor or campagna, and in the horizon a reddish yellow afterglow of sunset. There was one picture of a young girl telling her own fortune in the Italian fashion.

She is kneeling on a spot where the earth shows brown between tufts of short grass. The heart, cross, and anchor of hammered silver, which she has taken from her necklace, are scattered on the ground. Now she is lying on her knees, her eyes closed in good faith with one hand covering them, the other reaching down, seeking rapture of love beyond words, bitter sorrow solaced by the cross, or the trusting hope of a common fate. She has not yet dared to touch the ground. Her hand shrinks back in the cold, mysterious shadow; her cheeks are flushed, and her mouth trembles between prayer and tears. There is a solemnity in the air; the sunset glow threatens, hot and fierce out there in the distance, but softly melancholy where it steals in over the heather. "If you only knew — rapture of love beyond words, bitter sorrow solaced by the cross, or the trusting hope of a common fate?"

There was another in which she stands erect on the brown heath, tense with longing, her cheek pressed down on her folded hands. She is so sweet in her naïve longing and a wee bit sad and angered with life for passing her by. Why does not Eros come with kissing roses? Does he think she is too young? Ah, if he would only feel her heart, how it beats! If he would only lay his hand there! A world is in there, a world of worlds, if it would only awaken. But why does it not call? It is there like a bud, tightly folded around it own sweetness and beauty, existing only for itself, oppressed by itself.

For it knows there is something in life that it does not know. It is that which has warmed the sheltering petals and given light to the innermost heart of reddest dusk, where the scent lies yet scentless, a foreboding only, pressed into one tremulous tear!

Will it never be freed and breathe out all its slumbering fragrance, never to be rich in its own wealth? Will it never, never unfold and blush itself awake with gleaming rays of sunlight darting in under its petals? She has no patience anymore with Eros! Her lips are quivering with approaching tears; her eyes look out into space with hopeless defiance, and the little head sinks more and more forlornly, turning the delicate profile in toward the picture, where a gentle breeze wafts the reddish dust over dark green broom against a sherry-golden sky.

That was the way Erik painted. What he had to say always found expression in pictures such as these. He would sometimes dream in other images and long to break through that narrow circle within which he created, but when he had strayed beyond his bounds and tried his powers in other fields, he always returned with a chill sense of discouragement, feeling that he had been borrowing from others and producing something not his own. After these unfortunate excursions — which, however, always taught him more than he was aware of — he became more intensely Erik Refstrup than ever before. Then he would abandon

himself with more reckless courage and with almost poignant fervor to
the cult of his own individuality, while his whole manner of associating
with himself, to his slightest act, would be suffused with a religious
enthusiasm. He seemed surrounded by shadowy throngs of beautiful
forms, younger sisters of the slender-limbed women of Parmigianino
with their long necks and large, narrow princess hands; they sat at his
table, poured his wine with movements full of noble grace, and held
him in the spell of their fair dreams with Luini's mystic, contemplative
smile, so inscrutably subtle in its enigmatic sweetness.

But when he had served the god faithfully for eleven days, it sometimes happened that other powers gained the ascendancy over him, and
he would be seized with a violent craving for the coarse enjoyment of
gross pleasures. Then he would plunge into dissipations, feverish with
that human thirst for self-destruction which yearns, when the blood
burns as hotly as blood can burn, for degradation, perverseness, filth,
and smut, with precisely the measure of strength possessed by another
equally human longing, the longing to keep one's self greater than one's
self and purer.

In these moments there was but little that was rough and coarse
enough for him, and when they had passed, it was long before he could
regain his balance; for in truth these excesses were not natural to him;
he was too healthy for them, too little poisoned by brooding. In a sense,
they came as a rebound from his devotion to the higher spirits of his
art, almost like a revenge, as though his nature had been violated by the
pursuit of those idealistic aims which choice, aided by circumstances,
had made his own.

This twofold struggle, however, was not carried on along such definite
lines that it appeared on the surface of Erik Refstrup's life; nor did he
feel the need of making his friends understand him in this phase. No,
he was the same simple, happy-go-lucky fellow as of old, slightly awkward in his shrinking from emotions put into words, a little of a
freebooter in his capacity for seizing and holding. Yet the other thing
was in him and could be sensed sometimes in quiet moments, like the
bells that ring in a sunken city on the bottom of the sea. He and Niels
had never understood each other so well as now; both felt it, and silently
each renewed the old friendship. And when vacation time came, and
Niels felt that he really must make his long deferred visit to his Aunt
Rosalie, who was married to Consul Claudi in Fjordby, Erik went with
him.

The main highway from the richest district above Fjordby enters the
town between two great thorn hedges, which bound Consul Claudi's
vegetable garden and his large pleasure garden by the shore. What then
becomes of the road — whether it ends in the Consul's courtyard, which

is as large as a market place, or whether it is continued in a bend running between his hayloft and his lumberyard to form, later, the main street of the town — is a matter of opinion. Many travelers follow the bend and drive on, but there are also many who stop and think the goal reached when they have come within the Consul's wide tarred gateway, where the doors are always thrown back and covered with skins spread for drying.

The buildings on the premises were all old with the exception of the tall warehouse with its dead looking slate roof, the newest architectural feature in Fjordby. The long, low main building appeared to be forced to its knees by three large gables, and was joined, in a dim corner, to the wing containing the kitchen and stables; in another lighter corner, to the warehouse. In the dark corner was the back door of the store, which formed, with the peasants' waiting room, the office, and the servants' hall, a rather dingy world of its own, where the mingled odor of cheap tobacco and moldy floors, of spices and dried codfish and wet wool, made the air so thick you could almost taste it. But when you had passed through the office with its pungent smoke of sealing wax and had reached the hall which formed the dividing line between the business and the family, a prevailing perfume of new millinery prepared you for the delicate scent in the living rooms. It was not the fragrance of any nosegay or of any real flower; it was the intangible memory-laden atmosphere which pervades a home, though no one can say whence it comes. Every home has its own, and it may suggest a thousand things — the smell of old gloves or new playing cards or open pianos — but it is always different. It may be stifled by incense, perfumes, or cigar smoke, but it cannot be killed; it always comes back unchanged and is there just as before. Here it was of flowers, not stock or roses or any other flower that can be named, but rather as one might fancy the scent of those fantastic, pale sapphire lilies that twine their blossoms around vases of old porcelain. And how well it went with those wide, low rooms with their heirloom furniture and their stiff, old-fashioned grace! The floors were white as only grandmothers' floors can be; the walls were in plain colors with a light tracery of garlands in delicate tints running under the ceiling, which had a stucco rose in the center. The doors were fluted and had knobs of shining brass in the shape of dolphins. The windows of small square panes were curtained with filmy net, white as snow, its fullness caught up and fastened with coquettish bows of colored ribbon, like the curtains of a bridal bed of Corydon and Phyllis. In the windowsill the flowers of bygone days bloomed in motley green crocks; there were blue agapanthus, blue Canterbury bells, fine-leaved myrtles, fiery red verbenas, and butterfly bright geraniums. But it was, after all, chiefly the furniture that gave character to the rooms: immovable tables with wide expanse of darkened mahogany; chairs with backs that curled round your figure; cabinets of every conceivable form, gigantic dressers inlaid with mythological scenes in light yellow wood — Daphne, Arachne, and Narcissus — or small secretaries with thin twisted legs and on every tiny drawer a mosaic of dendrite marble representing a lovely square house with a tree near by — all from the time before Napoleon. There were mirrors, too, the glass painted in white or bronze with designs of rushes and lotus plants floating on a bright sea. As for the sofa, it was not one of your trifling things on four legs designed for two persons; no, solid and massive it rose from the floor to form a veritable spacious terrace; flanking it on either side and built in one with the sofa, was a console-cupboard, on top of which a smaller cabinet rose with architectonic effect to the height of a man and held a precious old jar above the reach of careless hands. It was no wonder there were so many old things in the Consul's house, for his father and grandfather had rested and enjoyed the good things of life within these walls in the intervals of their work in lumberyard and office.

The grandfather, Berendt Berendtsen Claudi, whose name the firm still bore, had built the houses and had interested himself chiefly in the retail and produce trade. The father had worked up the lumberyard, bought farmland, built the hayloft, and laid out the gardens. The present Claudi had developed the grain trade and built the warehouse. He united with his mercantile business the activities of the English and the Hanoverian vice-consulates as well as a Lloyd's agency; and the grain and the Western Sea kept him so busy he could give only a very cursory supervision to the other branches of the work. He therefore divided the responsibility between an insolvent cousin and an old unmanageable steward, who would drive the Consul into a corner every little while by declaring that, whatever happened to the store, the farm must be attended to, and when he wanted to plow, they could take horses for hauling lumber wherever they pleased — his they couldn't have, so help him. But as the man was capable, there was nothing to be done but to put up with him.

Consul Claudi was in the early fifties, a man of substantial presence. His regular features, strong to the point of coarseness, would as readily harden to an expression of energy and cool astuteness as they would relax into a look almost lickerish as though relishing a savory tidbit; and he was, in fact, equally at home whether driving a bargain with shrewd peasants or arguing with a stubborn salvage gang, or whether sitting with greybearded sinners over the last bottle of port wine, listening to stories more than salacious or telling them with the picturesque frankness for which he was noted.

This, however, was not all of the man.

His training naturally made him feel that he was on alien ground when he ventured outside of purely practical questions, but he never tried to conceal his ignorance. Much less did it ever occur to him to give his opinion and demand that it be respected for the reason that he was a citizen of mature years and practical experience and a large taxpayer. On the contrary, he would often listen with a reverence that was almost touching when ladies and young men discussed such matters; now and then he would venture a modest question prefaced by elaborate excuses, which almost always elicited a scrupulously painstaking answer, and then he would express his thanks with all the courtesy which is so gracious in an older man thanking his juniors.

At certain favorable moments there could be something surprisingly fine about Consul Claudi, a wistful look in his clear brown eyes, a melancholy smile around his strong lips, a seeking, reminiscent note in his voice, as though he yearned for another and in his own eyes better world than that to which his friends and acquaintances consigned him, hide and hair.

The messenger between himself and this better world was his wife. She was one of those pale, gentle, virginal natures who have not the courage or perhaps not the impulse, to give out their love in such fullness that there is no shred of self left in their innermost soul. Even in the most fleeting moment they can never be so carried away by their feeling that they throw themselves in blind rapture under the chariot wheels of their idol. They cannot do it, but all else they can do for the beloved; they can fulfill the heaviest duties, are ready for the most grievous sacrifices, and do not flinch from any humiliation whatsoever. This is true of the best among them.

Mrs. Claudi was not called on to bear such trials. Nevertheless her marriage was not without its sorrows; for it was a matter of common knowledge in Fjordby that the Consul was not, or at least had not been until a few years ago, the most faithful husband, and that he had several illegitimate children in the neighborhood.

This was, of course, a bitter grief to her, and it had not been easy to keep her heart steadfast through the tumult of jealousy, scorn and anger, shame and sickening fear, which had made her feel as though the ground were slipping away under her feet. But she stood firm. Not only did she never allow a reproachful word to pass her lips, but she warded off any confessions on the part of her husband, any direct prayer for forgiveness, and anything that might seem like a repentant vow. She felt that if it were ever put into words, they might sweep her along and away from him. Silently she would bear it, and in the silence she tried to make herself believe that she was in part to blame for her husband's crime, because of the barrier she had built around herself, which her love had not been strong enough to break down. She succeeded in magnifying this sin until she felt an indistinct need of forgiveness, and in course of time she brought herself to the point where she gave rise to a rumor that the girls whom Consul Claudi had seduced and their children were taken care of in other ways than with money; it seemed that a hidden woman's hand must be sheltering them, keeping them from harm, supporting them and guiding them.

So it came to pass that evil was turned into good, and a sinner and a saint each made the other better.

The Claudis had two children, a son who was in a merchant's office in Hamburg and a nineteen-year-old daughter named Fennimore after the heroine in *St. Roche,* one of Frau von Palzow's novels which had been very popular in the time of Mrs. Claudi's girlhood.

Fennimore and the Consul came down to meet the steamer on the day it brought Niels and Erik to Fjordby. Niels was pleasantly surprised to see that his cousin was pretty, for hitherto he had known her only from a terrible old family daguerreotype, where she appeared in a misty atmosphere, forming a group with her brother and her parents, all with hectic crimson on their cheeks and bright gilding on their jewelry. And now he found her simply lovely as she stood there in her light morning dress and her dainty little shoes with their black ribbons crossing a white-stockinged instep. She was resting one foot on the plank at the edge of the pier, and bent forward smiling to give him her parasol handle for a handshake and a welcome, before the steamer was made fast. Her lips were so red and her teeth so white, and her forehead and temples so delicately outlined under the wide brim of her Eugenie hat, from which shadowing edges of deep black lace fell weighted with bright jet.

At last the gangplank was let down, and the Consul started off with Erik. He had already introduced himself with twelve feet of water between them and, still shouting, had drawn Erik into a humorous conversation about the agonies of seasickness, which he carried on with a wizened hatter's widow on board. Now he was calling him to admire the large linden trees outside of the revenue collector's house and the new schooner standing ready to be launched from Thomas Rasmussen's shipyard.

Niels walked with Fennimore. She pointed to the flag flying in the garden in honor of him and his friend, and then they began to discuss the Neergaards in Copenhagen. They quickly agreed that Mrs. Neergaard was a little — a very little — they would not say the word, but Fennimore smiled primly and made a catlike movement with her hand. The characterization was evidently plain enough to them both, for they smiled and quickly became serious again. Silently they walked on, each wondering how he or she appeared in the other's eyes.

Fennimore had imagined Niels Lyhne taller, more distinguished, and of an individuality more marked — like an underscored word. He, on the other hand, had found much more than he expected. He thought her charming, almost alluring, in spite of her dress which savored too much of small town elegance. When they had entered the hall, and she stood looking down with a preoccupied air, as she took off her hat and smoothed her hair with wonderfully soft, languid, graceful turns of hand and wrist, he felt as grateful as if her movements had been caresses. This almost puzzling sense of gratitude did not leave him either that day or the next, and sometimes it welled up so strong and warm that he felt it would have been the greatest happiness if he might have thanked her in words for being so pretty and so sweet.

Very soon Erik as well as Niels felt quite at home in the Consul's hospitable house. Before many days they had slipped into that pleasantly arranged idling which is the real vacation life and which it is so difficult to guard against the friendly encroachments of well-meaning people. They had to use all their diplomacy to avoid the stuffy evening parties, large boating excursions, summer balls, and amateur theatricals which were constantly threatening their peace. They were ready to wish that the Consul's house and garden had been on a desert island; and Robinson Crusoe was not more agitated by fear on finding the footsteps in the sand than they were at the sight of strange paletots in the hall or unfamiliar reticules on the sitting room table. They much preferred to be by themselves; for they had scarcely passed the middle of the first week before they were both in love with Fennimore. It was not the mature passion which must and will know its fate and longs to have and to hold and to be assured. As yet it was only the first dawn of love like a hint of spring in the air, instinct with a longing akin to sadness and with an unrest that is gently pulsing joy. The heart is so tender and yielding and easily moved. A light on the water, a rustling in the leaves, a flower unfolding its petals — all seem to have a strange new power. Vague hopes without a name burst out, suddenly flooding the earth with sunlight and as suddenly vanishing again: weak despondency sails like a broad cloud over the glory, churning the flashes of hope down into its own grey wake. — Then hopelessness, melting hopelessness; bittersweet resignation to fate, a heart full of self-pity, renunciation gazing at its own reflection in quiet elegies and fainting in a sigh that is half dissembled. . . . But again there is the whispering of roses: a dreamland rises from the mist with golden haze over soft beech crowns and with fragrant summer darkness under leafy boughs arched over paths that lead no one knows whither.

One evening after tea they were all gathered in the sitting room. The garden and all outdoor amusements were barred, for the rain was pouring down; but no one seemed to mind. The sense of being shut in gave the room something of the snug comfort of a winter evening, and moreover the rain was a blessing. Everything had been so parched and dry, but now the water streamed down, and when the heavy drops rattled against the frame of the reflector in the window the sound called up vague, fleeting glimpses of luscious green meadows and freshened foliage. Now and then someone would say under his breath: "How it pours!" and glance at the windowpanes with a little gleam of pleasure and a half-conscious luxuriating in fellow feeling with everything out of doors. Erik had fetched the mandolin he had brought with him from Italy and sang about Napoli and the bright stars. Then a young lady who had been to tea sat down at the piano and accompanied her own rendering of "My little nook among the mountains," in Swedish, making the *atis* very broad to get the right Swedish effect.

Niels, who was not particularly musical, let himself be soothed into a gentle melancholy and sat lost in his own thoughts, until Fennimore began to sing.

Then he awoke, but not pleasantly.

Her song agitated him uncomfortably. She was no longer the little country girl when she gave herself up to the spell of her own voice. Strange how she let herself be carried away by the tones, how freely and unreservedly she poured herself into them! He felt it almost as something immodest, as though she were singing herself naked before him. There was a burning around his heart; his temples throbbed, and he cast his eyes down. Did none of the others see it? No, they saw nothing. Why, she had flown out of herself, away from Fjordby, from Fjordby poetry and Fjordby sentiments! She was in another and a bolder world, where the passions grew on high mountains and flung their red blossoms to the storm.

Could it be his lack of musical sense that made him read so much meaning into her song? He could hardly persuade himself that it was so, and yet he wished it, for he would much rather have her as she usually appeared. When she sat at her sewing, talking in her quiet, tranquil voice, or looking up with her clear, kind eyes, his whole being was drawn to her with the irresistible strength of a deep, calm longing for home. He wanted to humble himself before her, to bend the knee and call her holy. He always felt a strange yearning to come close to her, not only to her present self, but to her childhood and all the days he had not known her. When they were alone, he would lead her to talk of the past, of her little troubles and mistakes and the vagaries that every childhood is full of. He lived in these memories and clung to them with a restless jealousy and a languishing desire to possess and be one with these pale foreshadowings of a life which was even now glowing in richer, riper colors. And then came this song so strangely powerful! It startled him very much like a wide sweep of horizon suddenly revealed by a turn of the path, reducing the forest dell which had been his home to a mere corner in the landscape, and making its rippling lines seem insignificant beside the grandeur of the hills and distant moors. — Oh, but the landscape was a Fata Morgana, and what he thought he heard in her song only a fantasy; for now she spoke just as she always did and was her blessed self again. Moreover, he knew from a thousand little things that she was like still water, without storm or waves, reflecting the starry blue heavens.

It was thus he loved her, and thus he saw her; and when she was with him she gradually formed herself upon his image of her, not with any conscious dissembling, for after all his conception was partly true, and it was only natural — when his every word and look, his every thought and dream, appealed to that side of her nature and did homage to it — that she should assume the guise he almost forced upon her. Besides, how could she bother about giving each and everyone a correct impression of herself when all her thoughts centered around the one, Erik, the only one, her chosen lord, whom she loved with a passion that was not of herself and with an idolatrous worship that terrified her. She had imagined love to be a sweet dignity, not this consuming unrest, full of fear and humiliation and doubt. Many a time when the declaration seemed trembling on Erik's lips, she had felt as if it were her duty to put her hand on his mouth and warn him against speaking, accusing herself and telling him how she had deceived him and how unworthy of his love she was, how earthly and small and impure, so far from noble, so wretchedly low and common and wicked! She felt herself dishonest under his admiring gaze; calculating, when she failed to avoid him; criminal, when she could not bring herself to beg God in her evening prayer that He would turn Erik's heart from her in order that his life might be all sunlight and honor and glory. For she knew that her lowborn passion would drag him down.

It was almost in spite of himself that Erik loved her. His ideal had always been high, proud, and noble, with quiet melancholy suffusing her pale features and coolness of temple air lingering in the severe folds of her garment. But Fennimore's sweetness conquered him. He could not resist her beauty. There was such a fresh, innocent sensuousness about her whole form. When she walked her gait whispered of her body; there was a nakedness in her movements and a dreamy eloquence in her repose, neither of which she could help, for she could not conceal the one or silence the other, even had she been in the slightest degree conscious of their existence. No one saw this better than Erik, and he was fully aware of what a large part her purely physical beauty played in her attraction for him. He struggled against it, for there were exalted ideals of love in his soul, ideals which had their source, perhaps, not only in tradition and poetry, but in deeper strata of his nature than those that appeared on the surface. But whatever their source, they had to yield.

He had not yet confessed his love to Fennimore, when it happened that the good ship *Berendt Claudi* came in. Inasmuch as it was going to unload farther up the fjord, it did not enter the harbor, but lay out in the stream, and as the Consul was very proud of his schooner and wanted to show it to his guests, they rowed out there one afternoon to drink tea on board.

It was a glorious day without a breath of wind, and all were intent on a merry time. The hours passed quickly. They drank English porter, set their teeth in English hardtack as large as moons, and ate salted mackerel caught on the voyage across the North Sea. They pumped with the ship's pump till the water frothed, tipped the compass, drew water from the casks with the large tin siphon, and listened to the mate playing his octagonal hand harmonica.

It was quite dark before they were ready to return.

They separated into two parties. Erik and Fennimore and two of the older people went in the ship's yawl, which was to make a detour around the harbor and then row slowly to land, while the rest of the party went in the Consul's own boat, which was to steer directly for the pier. This arrangement was made in order to hear how the song would sound over the water on such a quiet night. Erik and Fennimore therefore sat together in the stern of the yawl and had the mandolin between them, but the singing was forgotten when the oars were dipped in the water and revealed an unusually bright phosphorescence which absorbed their attention.

Silently the boat glided onward, and behind it the dull, glassy surface was fluted with shifting lines and rings of a tender white light too faint to penetrate the darkness beyond its own groove, except now and then when it seemed to give out a luminous mist. It frothed white where the oars cut into it and slid backward in tremulous rings growing fainter and fainter; it was scattered from the blades in bright drops falling like a phosphorescent rain, which was extinguished in the air but lighted the water drop by drop. There was such quiet over the fjord that the sound of the oars seemed only to measure the stillness in pauses of equal length. Hushed and soft, the grey twilight brooded over the soundless deep; the boat and its occupants melted together in one dark mass, from which the phosphorescence freed the plying oars and sometimes a trailing rope's end, or perhaps the brown impassive face of the oarsman. No one spoke. Fennimore was cooling her hand in the water; she and Erik sat turning back to look at the network of light that trailed silently after the boat and held their thoughts in its fair meshes.

A call for a song shouted from land roused them, and together they sang two or three Italian romances to the accompaniment of the mandolin.

Then all was still again.

At last they landed at the little jetty running out from the garden. The Consul's empty boat was moored alongside, and the party had already gone up to the house. Fennimore's aunt and her companion followed them, but Erik and Fennimore remained standing and looked after the boat as it returned to the ship. The latch of the garden gate fell with a click; the sound of the oars grew fainter and fainter, and the swelling of the water around the pier died away. Then a breath stirred in the dark trees around them like a sigh that had hidden itself and now softly lifted the leaves, flew away, and left them alone.

In the same moment they turned to each other and away from the water. He caught her hand and slowly, questioningly, drew her close and kissed her. "Fennimore!" he whispered, and they walked through the dark garden.

"You have known it long!" he said, and she replied, "Yes." Then they walked on, and the latch fell once more.

Erik could not sleep when he reached his room at last, after drinking coffee with the company and saying good night at the street door.

There was no air in there; he flung the windows wide open, then threw himself on the couch and listened.

He wanted to get out again.

How everything resounded through the house! He could hear the Consul's slippers, and now Mrs. Claudi opened the kitchen door to see if the fire was out. What in the world could Niels want in his trunk this time of night! Ah — there was a mouse behind the wainscoting. Now someone crossed the attic in stocking feet — now another — there were two. — At last! He opened the door to the guest room within and listened, then he carefully opened the window, straddled over the sill, and slid into the courtyard. He knew that he could get down to the shore through the mangling room. If anyone saw him, he meant to say that he had forgotten his mandolin down by the jetty and wanted to rescue it from the dew. Therefore he slung the mandolin on his back.

The garden was a little lighter now; there was a slight breeze and a bit of moon which had laid a tremulous strip of silver from the jetty out to the *Berendt Claudi*.

He went through the garden out on the stone sloping which protected it from the water, running in abrupt angles round a large embankment and all the way out to the end of the harbor mole. Balancing uncomfortably on the flat, slanting stones, he finally reached the molehead and, rather out of breath, sat down on the bench.

Above his head the red lantern of the harbor light swung slowly back and forth with a sound like the sighing of iron, while the flag line flapped gently against its staff.

The moon had come out a little more and cast a cautious greyish-white light over the quiet ships in the harbor and over the maze of rectangular roofs and white dark-eyed gables in the town. Above and beyond it all the church steeple rose, calm and light.

He leaned back dreaming, while a wave of unutterable joy and exultation surged through his heart; he felt rich and full of strength and the warmth of life. It seemed as though Fennimore must hear every love thought that grew from his rapture, vine in vine, and blossom on blossom; and he rose, and quickly striking the strings of the mandolin sang triumphantly to the town asleep in there:

"Wakeful aloft lies my lassie,
  She listens to my song!"

Again and again, when his heart grew too full, he repeated the words of the old ballad.

Gradually he became calmer. Memories of the hours in the past when he had felt weakest, poorest, and most forlorn pressed in on him with a slight, tense pain like that of the first tears welling up in the eyes. He sat down on the bench again, and with his hand lying mute on the mandolin strings, he gazed out over the blue-grey expanse of the fjord, where the moon bridge formed a glittering way past the dark ship to the lines of the Morso hills, drawn in faint, melancholy cloud-blue land through a haze of white.

And the memories thronged, but they grew gentler, were lifted to fairer lands, and seemed lighted by a roseate dawn.

. . . My lassie!

He sang it to himself:

"Wakeful aloft lies my lassie,
  She listens to my song."

Chapter XI

*T*hree years had passed; Erik and Fennimore had been married for two years, and made their home in a little villa at Mariagerfjord. Niels had not seen Fennimore since that summer at Fjordby. He lived in Copenhagen and went out a great deal, but had no intimate friends except Dr. Hjerrild, who called himself old because touches of grey had begun to appear in his dark hair.

That unexpected engagement had been a hard blow to Niels. It had a benumbing effect on him. He grew more bitter and less confiding, and had no longer so much enthusiasm to pit against Hjerrild's pessimism. Though he still pursued his studies, their plan was less and less definite, while his purpose of some time completing them and beginning his real lifework flickered uncertainly. He lived much among people, but very little with them. They interested him, but he did not in the least care to have them be interested in him; for he felt the force that should have driven him to do his part with the others or against them slowly ebbing out of him. He could wait, he told himself, even if he had to wait till it was too late. Whoever has faith is in no hurry — that was his excuse to himself. For he believed that, when he came down to the bedrock of his own nature, he did have faith strong enough to move mountains — the trouble was that he never managed to set his shoulder to them. Once in a while, the impulse to create welled up in him, and he longed to see a part of himself freed in work that should be his very own. For days he would be excited with the happy, titanic effort of carting the clay for his Adam, but he never formed it in his own image. The will power necessary to persistent self-concentration was not in him. Weeks would pass before he could make up his mind to abandon the work, but he did abandon it, asking himself, in a fit of irritation, why he should continue. What more had he to gain? He had tasted the rapture of conception; there remained the toil of rearing, cherishing, nourishing, carrying to perfection — Why? For whom? He was no pelican, he told himself. But argue as he might, he was dissatisfied with himself and felt that he had not fulfilled his own expectations; nor did it avail him to carp at these expectations and ask whether they were well founded. He had reached the point where he had to choose, for when first youth is past — early or late in accordance with each person's individuality — then, early or late, dawns the day when Resignation comes to us as a temptress, luring us to forego the impossible and be content. And Resignation has much in her favor; for how often have not the idealistic aspirations of youth been beaten back, its enthusiasms been shamed, its hopes laid waste! — The ideals, the fair and beautiful, have lost nothing of their radiance, but they no longer walk here among us as in the early days of our youth. The broad, firmly planted stairway of worldly wisdom has conveyed them back, step by step, to that heaven whence our simpler faith once brought them down; and there they sit, radiant but distant, smiling, but weary, in divine quiescence, while the incense of a slothful adoration rises, puff on puff, in festive convolutions.

Niels Lyhne was tired. These repeated runnings to a leap that was never leaped had wearied him. Everything seemed to him hollow and worthless, distorted and confused, and, oh, so petty! He preferred to stop his ears and stop his mouth and to immerse himself in studies that had nothing to do with the busy everyday world, but were like an ocean apart, where he could wander peacefully in silent forests of seaweed among curious animals.

He was tired, and the root of his weariness sprang from his baffled hope of love; thence it had spread, quickly and surely, through his whole being, to all his faculties and all his thoughts. Now he was cold and passionless enough, but in the beginning, after the blow had fallen, his love had grown, day by day, with the irresistible power of a malignant fever. There had been moments when his soul was almost bursting with insane passion; it swelled like a wave in its infinite longing and frothing desire; it rose and went on rising and rising, till every fiber in his brain and every cord in his heart were strung tense to the breaking point. Then weariness had come, soothing and healing, making his nerves dull against pain, his blood too cold for enthusiasm, and his pulse too weak for action. And more than that, it had protected him against a relapse by giving him all the prudence and egoism of the convalescent. When his thoughts went back to those days in Fjordby, he had a sense of immunity akin to the feeling of a man who has just passed through a severe illness and knows that now, when he has endured his allotted agony, and the fever has burned itself to ashes within him, he will be free for a long, long time.

Then it happened, one summer day, after Erik and Fennimore had been married for two years, that he received a half whining, half boasting letter from Erik, in which he blamed himself for having wasted his time of late. He did not know what the matter was, but he had no ideas. The people he met in the neighborhood were fine, jolly fellows, no conventionality or nonsense about them, but they were perfect dromedaries with regard to art. There was not a human being he could talk with, and he had gotten himself into a slough of laziness and stagnation which he could not pull out of. He never had a glimmering of an idea or a mood, and never felt inspired. Sometimes he was afraid that his power had run out, and that he never would do anything anymore. But this could not possibly go on forever! It must come back; he had been too rich to end like this, and when it came he would show them what art was, those fellows who painted away all the time as if they had learned it by rote. For the present, however, he was as if bewitched, and it would be an act of friendship if Niels would visit Mariagerfjord. They would make him as comfortable as circumstances allowed, and he could just as well spend his vacation there as any other place. Fennimore sent her love and would be glad to see him.

This letter was so unlike Erik that Niels saw at once there must be something serious amiss or he would not complain in this fashion. He was aware, too, of how little volume there was in the wellspring of Erik's production — a slender stream only, which unfavorable circumstances could easily dry out. He would go at once! For all that had happened, Erik should find him a faithful friend; whatever the years had loosened of old ties and uprooted of old illusions, he would at least know how to guard this old friendship of their childhood. He had helped Erik before, and he would help him now. A fanaticism of friendship possessed him. He would renounce his future, fame, ambitious dreams, everything, for Erik's sake. All that he owned of smoldering enthusiasm and creative ferment should be Erik's; he would merge himself in Erik with his whole self and all his ideas, holding nothing back, keeping nothing for himself. He dreamed of greatness for the friend who had torn his life asunder so roughly, and saw himself blotted out, forgotten, impoverished, deprived of his intellectual heritage; and he went on dreaming that his gift to Erik should become no longer a loan, but Erik's very own, as he coined it into works and deeds and gave it his stamp. Erik in honor and glory, and he himself one of the many, many commonplace folk and nothing else; poor, at last, by necessity, not by choice; a real beggar, not a prince in disguise . . . And it was sweet to dream himself so bitterly humble.

But dreams are dreams, and he laughed at himself, as he thought that people who neglect their own work always have no end of time to interest themselves in that of others. It also occurred to him that, when he came face to face with Erik, the latter would, of course, disclaim his letter and pass it off as a joke. He certainly would think it extremely absurd if Niels were actually to present himself with the announcement that he was ready to help him recover his creative power. Nevertheless he went. In his inmost heart he believed that he could do some good, and no matter how much he tried to explain it away or cast doubts upon it, he could not rid himself of the feeling that it really was the friendship of their boyhood which had reasserted itself in all its old simplicity and warmth, in spite of the years and what the years had brought.

The villa at Mariagerfjord belonged to an elderly couple who had been forced by ill health to make their home in the south for an indefinite period. They had not intended to rent the place, as they had started out with the idea of returning after six months, and therefore had left everything just as it was. So when Erik leased the house fully furnished, this was so literally true that he got it with bric-à-brac, family portraits, and everything else, even to an attic full of decrepit furniture with old letters in the drawers of the secretaries.

Erik had discovered the villa when he left Fjordby after his engagement. As it contained everything they needed, and as he hoped to go to Italy in a year or two, he had persuaded Consul Claudi to postpone the purchase of household furnishings for a while. They had moved into Marianelund very much as into a hotel, except that they brought a few more trunks than travelers usually carry.

The house fronted the fjord, less than twenty feet from the water, and was rather ordinary in appearance. It had a balcony above, a veranda below, and at the back a young garden with trees no thicker than walking sticks, but from the garden one could step right into a magnificent bit of beech woods with heathery glades and wide clefts opening between banks of white clay, and that made up for many shortcomings.

This was Fennimore's new home, and for a while it was as bright as happiness could make it, for they were both young and in love, strong and healthy, and without a care for their means of subsistence, either spiritual or material.

But every palace of joy that rises heavenward has sand mixed in the earth on which it is founded, and the sand will collect and run away, slowly perhaps, imperceptibly perhaps, but it runs and runs, grain by grain . . . And love? Even love is not a rock, however much we may wish to believe it.

She loved him with her whole soul, with the hot tremulous passion born of fear. He was to her much more than a god, much nearer — he was an idol, whom she worshiped without reason and without reserve.

His love was strong as hers, but it lacked the fine, manly tenderness that protects the loved woman against herself and watches over her dignity. Dimly he felt it as a duty, which called him sometimes in a faint, low voice, but he would not hear. She was too alluring in her blind love; her beauty, which had the provocative luxuriance and the humble seductiveness of the female slave, incited him to a passion that knew neither bounds nor mercy.

In the old myth about Amor, is it not told somewhere that he puts his hand over Psyche's eyes before they fly away, rapturously, into the glowing night?

Poor Fennimore! If she could have been consumed by the fire of her own heart, he who should have guarded her would have fanned the flames; for he was like that drunken monarch who swung the incendiary torch, shouting with joy to see his imperial city burn, intoxicating himself with the sight of the leaping flames, until the ashes made him sober.

Poor Fennimore! She did not know that the hymn of joy can be sung so often that both melody and words are lost, and nothing remains but a twaddle of triviality. She did not know that the intoxication which uplifts today takes its strength from the wings of tomorrow, and when at length sobriety dawned, grey and heavy, she realized tremblingly that they had loved themselves down to a sweet contempt for themselves and each other — a sweet contempt which day by day lessened in sweetness and became, at last, utterly bitter. They turned away from each other as far as they could; he, to dream about his betrayed ideal of lofty coldness and scornful grace; she, to gaze with longing despair at the dim, quiet shores of her girlhood days, now so immeasurably far away. With each day that passed, it seemed harder to bear; shame burned madly in her veins, and a suffocating disgust with herself made everything seem wretched and hopeless. There was a small deserted room containing nothing but the trunks she had brought from home, and there she would often sit, hour after hour, until the sun sank over the world out there and filled the room with reddish light. There she tortured herself with thoughts sharper than thorns and scourged herself with words more stinging than whips, until she was stupefied by misery and tried to deaden her pain by throwing herself down on the floor as something too full of corruption and dregs — a carrion of herself — too foul to be the seat of a soul. Her husband's mistress! That thought was never out of her mind; with that she threw herself in the dust and trampled on herself; with that she barred every hope of regeneration and turned every happy memory to stone.

Gradually a hard, brutal indifference came over her, and she ceased to despair, as she had long ceased to hope. Her heaven had fallen, but she did not try to raise the vault again in her dreams. The earth was good enough for her, since she was but of earth, earthy. She did not hate Erik, nor did she draw away from him. No, she accepted his kisses; she despised herself too much to repulse them, and besides, was she not his wife — his woman?

For Erik, too, the awakening was bitter, although his man's prosaic common sense had warned him that some time it must come. When it really came, however, when love no longer gave boot for every bane, and the veil of gleaming gold in which it had descended to earth for him had been wafted away, he felt such a sinking of his spirits and such a sluggishness creeping over all his powers that he was angered and alarmed. Feverishly he turned to his work to assure himself that he had lost nothing else besides happiness, but art did not give him the answer he hoped for. He got hold of some unlucky ideas which he could not do anything with and yet could not make up his mind to abandon. Though they refused to take shape, they continued to tease his mind, and prevented other ideas from breaking through or absorbing his energy. He grew despondent and dissatisfied and sank into a moody idleness, since work was so confoundedly perverse, and since, of course, he had only to wait for the spirit to move him again. But time passed; his talent was still barren, and here by the quiet fjord there was nothing that could fructify it; nor were there any fellow artists whose triumphs could spur him on either to emulation or to creative opposition.

This inactivity grew unbearable. He was seized with a violent craving to feel himself, no matter how or in what, and since nothing else offered, he turned to a crowd of older and younger men about the neighborhood who enlivened the dullness of country life by such dissipations as their limited fancy could invent and their rather one-sided taste could savor. The kernel of their pleasures was always drinking and cards, no matter whether the shell enclosing them was called a market day or a hunt. Nor did it make any particular difference that the scene was occasionally laid in a small neighboring town, and certain real or imagined business was transacted with the tradesmen during the afternoon: for the bargain was always closed at night in the tavern, where the discriminating landlord always showed persons of the right stripe into Number Caveat. If there happened to be strolling players in town, the tradesmen were let go, for the players were more sociable, did not shy at the bottle, and were usually ready to undergo the miraculous — though never quite successful — cure of drinking themselves sober in gin after getting drunk on champagne.

The leader of the crowd was a hunting squire of sixty, and its main stock was made up of small landowners and country gentlemen in the neighborhood, though it also included a massive young dandy of a brandy distiller and a white-necked tutor, who had not been a tutor for twenty years or more, but had gone as a vagrant from house to house with a sealskin bag and an old grey mare, which he used to say he had bought from a horse butcher. He was a silent drinker, a virtuoso on the flute, and was supposed to know Arabic. Among those whom the squire called his "staff" were also a solicitor, who always had new stories to tell, and a doctor, who knew only a single one from the siege of Lübeck in the year 6.

The members of this band were widely scattered, and it scarcely ever happened that they were all together at one time, but whenever anyone stayed away from the company too long the squire would issue a summons to the faithful to inspect the renegade's oxen, which all understood to mean that they should quarter themselves upon the unfortunate man for two or three days and turn his house upside down with drinking, gambling, and whatever rustic amusements the season afforded. During such a punitive visit, it once happened that the whole party was snowbound, and the host's supply of coffee, rum, and sugar ran out, so that they were reduced to drinking a coffee punch boiled of chicory, sweetened with syrup, and strengthened with brandy.

It was a coarse-grained crowd of boon companions that Erik had fallen in with, but perhaps people of such tremendous animal vitality could hardly find sufficient outlet in more civilized amusements, and their unfailing good humor and broad, bruinlike joviality really took away much of the grossness. If Erik's talent had been akin to that of Brouwer or Ostade, this choice band of revelers would have been a perfect gold mine to him. As it was, he got nothing out of it except that he enjoyed it very much, too much in fact, for soon this wild racketing became indispensable to him and took up nearly all his time. Now and then, he would blame himself for his idling and vow to end it, but whenever he made an attempt at working, the sense of blackness and spiritual impotence would come over him again and drive him back to the old life.

The letter to Niels had been framed one day when his everlasting barrenness had made him wonder if his talent had been attacked by a wasting disease. As soon as it was sent, he regretted it, and hoped that Niels would let his plaint go in at one ear and out at the other.

But Niels he came, the knight-errant of friendship personified, and was met with that mixture of rebuff and pity which knights-errant in all times have encountered from those in whose behalf they have dragged Rosinante out of her snug stable. As Niels was tactful, however, and bided his time, Erik thawed before long, and the old intimacy was soon established between them; for Erik's need of pouring himself out in complaint and confession had grown into an almost physical craving.

One evening after bedtime, when Fennimore had retired, they sat over their cognac and water in the dark sitting room. Only the glow of their cigars showed where they were, and once in a while, when Niels leaned far back in his chair, his upturned profile would stand out black against the dark windowpane. They had been drinking a good deal, Erik especially, while they sat talking of the time when they were boys at Lönborggaard. Now Fennimore's departure had made a pause which neither of them seemed inclined to break, for their thoughts came stealing upon them in a pleasant languor, as they listened drowsily to the singing of their blood, warm from the cognac.

"What fools we were when we were twenty," came Erik's voice at last. "God knows what we expected and how we had got it into our heads that such things were on earth. We called them by the same names that they bear in reality, but we meant something entirely above and beyond comparison with this tame sufficiency that we've got. There isn't much to life, really. Do you think so?"

"Oh, I don't know; I take it for what it is worth. We don't generally live very much. Most of the time we only exist. If you could get life handed to you in one whole large, appetizing cake that you could set your teeth in . . . but doled out in bits! — no, it's not amusing."

"Tell me, Niels — it's only to you I can talk of such absurd things; I don't know how it is, but you're so queer. Tell me — is there anything in your glass? All right! — Have you ever thought of death?"

"Have I? Why, yes. Have you?"

"I don't mean at funerals or when a man is sick, but sometimes when I'm just sitting here comfortably it comes over me like — like a despair simply. When I sit here and mope and don't do anything and *can't* do anything, then I actually feel the time slipping away from me. Hours and weeks and months rush past with nothing in them, and I can't nail them to the spot with a piece of work. I don't know if you understand what I mean, but I want to get hold of it with something achieved. When I paint a picture, the time I use for it remains mine forever; it isn't lost, even though it's past. I am sick when I think of the days as they go — incessantly. And I *have* nothing, or I can't get at it. It's torture! I sometimes get into such a rage that I have to get up and walk the floor and sing some idiotic thing to keep myself from crying, and then when I stop I am almost mad to think that the time has gone meanwhile, and is going while I think, and going and going. There is nothing more wretched than to be an artist. Here I am, strong and healthy; I have eyes to see; my blood is warm and red; my heart beats, and there is nothing the matter with my head, and I *want* to work, but I can't. I am struggling and groping for something that eludes me, something that I can't grasp even if I toil and moil till I sweat blood. What can a man do for inspiration or to get an idea? Is it all one whether I concentrate or whether I go out and pretend I am not looking for anything, never, never anything except the sense that now Time is standing up to the waist in eternity and hauling in the hours, and they rush past, twelve white and twelve black, never stopping, never stopping. What shall I do? What do people do when they feel like that? Surely, I can't be the first. Have you nothing to suggest?"

"Travel."

"No, anything but that. What made you think of that? You don't believe I'm done for, do you?"

"Done for! No, but I thought the new impressions —"

"The new impressions! Exactly. Have you never heard about people who had plenty of talent in their first youth while they were fresh and full of hope and plans, but when youth had passed their talent was gone too — and never came back?"

They were silent for a long time.

"*They* traveled, Niels, to get new impressions, that was their fixed idea. The south, the Orient — it was all in vain; it slid off from them as from a looking glass. I have seen their graves in Rome — two of them, but there are many, many others. One of them went mad."

"I have never heard that about painters before."

"It's true. What can it be, do you think? A hidden nerve that's given way? Or something we have failed in or sinned against in ourselves, perhaps — who knows? A soul is such a fragile thing, and no one knows how far the soul extends in a human being. We ought to be good to ourselves — Niels!" His voice had grown low and soft. "I have often longed to travel, because I felt so empty. You have no idea how I have longed for it, but I simply don't dare to, for suppose it didn't help, and that I was one of those people I was telling you of. What then!

"Think of standing face to face with the certainty that I was done for, didn't possess anything, couldn't do anything — think of it — couldn't do anything! A paltry wretch, a cursed dog of a cripple, a miserable eunuch! What do you think would become of me? And after all it is not impossible. My first youth is past, and as for illusions and that sort of thing, I can assure you I haven't many left. It's terrible how we go through them, and yet I was never one of those who are anxious to get rid of them. I was not like you and the rest of the people who used to foregather at Mrs. Boye's — you were always so busy plucking the fine feathers from one another, and the balder you got, the more you crowed. Still what's the difference — sooner of later we all start molting."

They were silent again. The air was bitter with cigar smoke and heavy with cognac, and they sighed drearily, oppressed by the stuffiness of the room and by their own very sad hearts.

Niels had traveled two hundred miles to bring aid, and here he sat feeling his impulse put to shame, while the colder side of his nature looked on. For what could he do, when it came to the point? What if he tried to talk picturesquely to Erik, in many words of purple and ultramarine, dripping with light and wading in shadow! There had been a dream of something like that in his brain when he started out. How utterly absurd! To bring aid! You might perhaps drive away the goddess with the closed hands from an artist's door, but that was certainly the utmost; you could no more help him to create than you could help him, if he were paralyzed, to lift his little finger by his own strength. No, not though your heart overflowed with affection and sympathy and devotion and everything else that was generous . . . What you ought to do was to mind your own affairs; that was useful and healthy, but of course it was easier to let your heart run amuck in a large and generous way. The only trouble was that it was so lamentably impracticable and so utterly ineffective. Minding your own affairs and doing it well did not insure you paradise, but at least you did not have to cast down your eyes before either God or man.

Opportunity was abundant for Niels to make melancholy reflections on the impotence of a kind heart, for all that he accomplished was to keep Erik at home a little more than usual for a month or so. Nevertheless, he did not care to return to Copenhagen during the hot season, and as he did not wish to remain a guest indefinitely, he engaged a room with a family a little above the peasant class, on the opposite shore of the fjord, so near that he could row over to Marianelund in fifteen minutes. Now that he was accustomed to the neighborhood, he would just as lief stay there as any other place, for he was one of the susceptible people over whom outward surroundings easily acquire a hold. Besides, his friend and his cousin Fennimore were there, and that was reason enough, especially as there was not a human being anywhere else expecting him.

During the trip from Copenhagen, he had carefully thought out his behavior to Fennimore and how he would show her that he had forgotten so completely that he did not remember there was anything to forget; above all, no coldness, but a friendly indifference, a superficial cordiality, a polite sympathy; that was the proper attitude.

But it was all thrown away.

The Fennimore he met was a different person from the one he had left. She was still lovely; her form was luxuriant and beautiful as before, and she had the same slow, languid movements that charmed him in former days, but there was a dreary thoughtlessness in the expression of her mouth as of one who had thought too much, and a pitiful, tortured cruelty in her gentle eyes. He did not understand it at all, but one fact was at least clear, and that was that she had had other things to think of than remembering him, and that she was quite callous to any memories he could awaken. She looked like one who had made her choice and done the worst she could do with it.

Little by little, he began to spell and put things together, and one day, when they were walking along the shore, he began to understand.

Erik was cleaning up his studio, and as they were strolling by the water, the maid came out with an apronful of refuse which she threw out on the beach. There was a litter of old brushes, fragments of casts, broken palette knives, bits of oil bottles, and empty paint tubes. Niels poked the heap with his foot, and Fennimore looked on with the vague curiosity people often feel in turning over old rubbish. Suddenly Niels drew his foot away as if something had burned it, but caught himself as quickly, and gave the pile another kick.

"Oh, let me see it," begged Fennimore, and put her hand on his arm as if to stop him. He bent down and pulled out a plaster cast of a hand holding an egg.

"It must be a mistake," he said.

"Why no, it is broken," she replied quietly, as she took it from him. "See, the forefinger is gone," she added, pointing, but when she suddenly became aware that the egg had been cut in two and a yolk painted inside it with chrome yellow, she blushed, and, bending down, she slowly and deliberately knocked the hand against a stone, until it was broken into little bits.

"Do you remember the time it was cast?" Niels asked, in order to say something.

"I remember that my hand was smeared with green soap so the plaster should not stick to it. Is that what you were thinking of?"

"No, I mean the time when Erik passed the cast around at the tea table. Don't you remember, when it came to your old aunt, how her eyes filled with tears, and she embraced you with the deepest compassion and kissed you on the brow, as if some harm had been done to you?"

"Yes, people are so sensitive."

"No, we all laughed at her, but there was a delicacy in it nevertheless, although it was so nonsensical."

"Yes, there is much of that nonsensical delicacy in the world."

"I believe you want to quarrel with me today."

"No, I don't but there is something I want to say to you. You won't take offence at a little frankness? — Well, then — suppose a man tells a story that is not very nice in his wife's presence and perhaps otherwise shows what appears to you a lack of consideration for her; don't you think it is unnecessary for you then to express your protest by your emphatic fastidiousness and your exceeding great chivalry? It is fair to assume that the man knows his own wife best, and knows that it won't offend or wound her; otherwise he would not do it. Is not that true?"

"No, it is not true, generally speaking, but in this case, and on your authority, I don't mind saying yes."

"That's right. You may be sure that women are not the ethereal creatures many a good youth fancies; they are really no more delicate than men, and not very different from them. Take my word for it, there has been some filthy clay used in the shaping of them both."

"Dearest Fennimore! Thank God you don't know what you are saying, but you are very unjust to women and to yourself. I believe in woman's purity."

"Woman's purity! What do you mean by woman's purity?

"I mean — that is —"

"You mean — I will tell you; you mean nothing, for that is another piece of nonsensical delicacy. A woman can't be pure, and isn't supposed to be — how could she? It is against nature! And do you think God made her to be pure? Answer me! — No, and ten thousand times no. Then why this lunacy! Why fling us up to the stars with one hand, when you have to pull us down with the other! Can't you let us walk the earth by your side, one human being with another, and nothing more at all? It is impossible for us to step firmly on the prose of life when you blind us with your poetic will-o'-the-wisps. Let us alone! For God's sake, let us alone!"

She sat down and wept.

Niels understood much. Fennimore would have been miserable had she known how much. Was it not partly the old story of love's holiday fare which refuses to turn into daily bread, but goes on being holiday fare, only more tasteless, more insipid, and less nourishing, day by day? One can't perform a miracle, and the other can't perform it, and there they sit in their banqueting clothes, careful to smile the agony of hunger and thirst, while their eyes shrink from each other, and hatred begins to grow in their hearts. Was not that the first chapter, and was not the other the equally dreary tale of a woman's despair at not being able to recover herself after finding out that the demigod, whose bride she became so joyously, was only an ordinary mortal? First the despair, the bootless despair, and then the merciful stupor — that must be the explanation. It seemed to Niels that he understood everything: the hardness in her, the dreary humility, and her coarseness, which was the bitterest drop in the whole goblet. By degrees he came to see also that his delicacy and deferential homage must oppress and irritate her, because a woman who has been hurled from the purple couch of her dreams to the pavement below will quickly resent any attempt to spread carpets over the stones which she longs to feel in all their hardness. In her first despair she is not satisfied to tread the path with her feet: she is determined to crawl it on her knees, choosing the way that is steepest and roughest. She desires no helping hand and will not lift her head — let it sink down with its own heaviness, so that she may put her face to the ground and taste the dust with her tongue!

Niels pitied her with all his heart, but he left her alone as she desired.

It was hard to look on and not help, to sit apart and dream her happy, in stupid dreams, or to wait and calculate, with the cold knowledge of the physician, how long she had to suffer. He told himself, in this dreary wisdom, that there could be no relief until her old hope in the fair, gleaming treasures of life had bled to death and a more sluggish stream had entered her veins, making her dull enough to forget, blunt enough to accept, and, at last, at last, coarse enough to rejoice in the thick atmosphere of a bliss many heavens lower than that which she had meekly hoped and humbly prayed for wings to reach. — He was full of disgust with all the world when he thought that she, to whom he had once knelt in adoration, had come to such a pass that she had been forced to a slave's estate, and stood at the gate shivering with cold, while he rode past on his high horse with the large coins of life jingling in his pocket.

One Sunday afternoon, in the latter part of August, Niels rowed across the fjord. Fennimore was at home alone when he came; he found her lying on a sofa in the corner room, and very miserable. Her breath came with that low, monotonous moaning which seems to afford relief from pain, and she said that she had a frightful headache. There was no one to help her, for she had given the maid leave to go home to Hadssund, and soon afterward someone had come and carried off Erik; she could not understand where they had gone in the rain. Now she had been lying there for two hours trying to sleep, but it was impossible, the pain was so bad. She had never had it before, and it had come on so suddenly — at dinner time there had been nothing the matter. First it was in the temples, and then it seemed to dig deeper and deeper and deeper in; now it seemed to be behind her eyes — if it only was not anything dangerous. She was not used to being ill, and was very frightened and unhappy.

Niels comforted her as well as he could, telling her to lie still, close her eyes, and not speak. He found a heavy shawl, which he wrapped around her feet, fetched vinegar from the buffet, and made a cold compress, which he laid on her brow. Then he sat down quietly by the window, and looked out at the rain.

From time to time, he stole over to her on tiptoe and changed the compress without speaking, merely nodding to her, as she looked up at him gratefully between his hands. Sometimes she wanted to speak, but he hushed her with a look, shaking his head, and returned to his seat again.

At last she fell asleep.

One hour passed and another, and she was still sleeping. Slowly one quarter slipped into the other, while the melancholy daylight faded, and the shadows in the room waxed larger, as if they were growing out of the furniture and the walls. Outside the rain fell, evenly and steadily, blotting out every other sound in its low, incessant patter.

She was still sleeping.

The fumes of the vinegar and the vanilla scent of the heliotrope, mingling in a pungent odor like wine, filled the room. Warmed by their breath, the air covered the grey windowpanes with a dewy film, which grew denser with the increasing coolness of the evening.

By this time, he was far away in memories and dreams, though a part of his consciousness still watched over the sleeper and followed her sleep. Gradually, as the darkness pressed in, his fancy wearied of feeding these dreams that flickered up and died down, just as the soil gets tired of bringing forth the same crop again and again; and the dreams grew feebler, more sterile, and stiffer, losing the luxuriant details that had entwined them like long shoots of clinging vines. His thoughts left the distance and came homing back. — How quiet everything was! Was it not as if they were together, he and she, on an island of silence rising above the monotonous sea of sound made by the soft patter of the rain? And their souls were still, calm and safe, while the future seemed to slumber in a cradle of peace.

Would that it might never awaken, and that all might remain as now — no more happiness than that of peace, but neither any misery nor irking unrest! Would that the present might close as a bud closes around itself, and that no spring would follow!

Fennimore called. She had been lying awake for some time, too happy in being free from pain to think of speaking. Now she wanted to get up and light the lamp, but Niels continued to act as physician, and compelled her to lie still. It was not good for her to get up yet; he had matches and could easily find the lamp.

When he had lit it, he put it on the flower stand in the corner, where its milky white globe shone softly veiled by the delicate, slumbering leaves of an acacia. The room was just light enough so that they could see each other's face.

He sat down in front of her, and they spoke about the rain and said how lucky it was that Erik had taken his raincoat, and how wet poor Trine would be. Then their conversation came to a standstill.

Fennimore's thoughts were not quite awake yet, and in her weakness it seemed pleasant to lie thus musing without speaking. Nor was Niels inclined to talk, for he was still under the spell of the afternoon's long silence.

"Do you like this house?" Fennimore asked at last.

"Why yes, fairly well."

"Really? Do you remember the furniture at home?"

"At Fjordby? Yes indeed, perfectly."

"You don't know how I love it, and how I long for it sometimes. The things we have here don't belong to us — they are only rented — and have no association with anything, and we are not going to live with them any longer than we stay in this place. You may think it queer, but I assure you, I often feel lonely here among all these strange pieces of furniture that stand around here so indifferent and stupid and take me for what I am without caring the least bit about me. And as I know they are not going with me — that they will just stand here and be rented by other people — I can't get fond of them or interested in them as I should if I knew that my home would always be theirs, and that whatever came to me of good or ill would come in the midst of them. Do you think it childish? Perhaps it is, but I can't help it."

"I don't know what it is, but I have felt it too. When I was left alone abroad, my watch stopped, and when it came back from the watchmaker and was going as before, it was — just what you mean. I liked the feeling; there was something peculiar about it, something genuinely good."

"Yes indeed! Oh, I should have kissed it, if I had been you."

"Would you?"

"Do you know," she said suddenly, "you have never told me anything about Erik as a boy? What was he like?"

"Everything that is good and fine, Fennimore. Splendid, brave — a boy's ideal of a boy, not exactly a mother's or a teacher's ideal, but the other, which is so much better."

"How did you get along together? Were you very fond of each other?"

"Yes, I was in love with him, and he didn't mind — that is about how it was. We were very different. I always wanted to be a poet and become famous, but what do you suppose he said he wanted to be, one day when I asked him? — An Indian, a real red Indian with war paint and all the rest! I remember that I couldn't understand it at all. It was incomprehensible to me how anyone could want to be a savage — civilized creature that I was!"

"But was it not strange, then, that he should become an artist?" said Fennimore, and there was something cold and hostile in her tone, as she asked.

Niels noticed it with a little start. "Not at all," he answered; "it is really rare that people become artists with the whole of their nature. And such strong fellows overflowing with vitality like Erik often have an unutterable longing for what is fine-grained and delicate: for an exquisite virginal coldness, a lofty sweetness — I hardly know how to express it. Outwardly they may be robust and full-blooded enough, even coarse, and no one suspects what strange, romantic, sentimental secrets they carry about with them, because they are so bashful — spiritually bashful, I mean — that no pale little maiden can be more shy about her soul than are these big, hard-stepping menfolks. Don't you understand, Fennimore, that such a secret, which can't be told in plain words right out in common everyday air, may dispose a man to be an artist? And they can't express it in words, they simply can't; we have to believe that it is there and lives its quiet life within them, as the bulb lives in the earth; for once in a while they do send fragrant, delicately tinted flowers up to the light. Do you understand? — Don't demand anything for yourself of this blossoming strength, believe in it, be glad to nourish it and to know that it is there. — Forgive me, Fennimore, but it seems to me that you and Erik are not really good to each other. Can't you make a change? Don't think of who is right or how great the wrong is, and don't treat him according to his deserts — how would even the best of us fare if we got our deserts! No, think of him as he was in the hour when you loved him most; believe me, he is worthy of it. You must not measure and weigh. There are moments in love, I know, full of bright, solemn ecstasy, when we would give our lives for the beloved if need be. Is not that true? Remember it now, Fennimore, for his sake and your own."

He was silent.

She said nothing either, but lay very still with a melancholy smile on her lips, pale as a flower.

Then she half rose and stretched out her hand to Niels. "Will you be my friend?" she asked.

"I am your friend, Fennimore," and he took her hand.

"Will you, Niels?"

"Always," he replied, lifting the hand to his lips reverently.

When he rose, it seemed to Fennimore that he held himself more erect than she had ever seen him before.

A little later Trine came in to announce her return, and then there was tea, and at last the rowing back through the dreary rain.

Toward morning Erik came home, and when Fennimore saw him by the cold, truthful light of dawn, preparing to go to bed, heavy and unsteady with drink, his eyes glazed from gambling and his face dirty-pale after the sleepless night, then all the fair words Niels had spoken seemed to her quite visionary. The bright promises she had made to her own heart fainted and paled before the oncoming day — vapory dreams and fumes of fancy: a fairy flock of lies!

What was the use of struggling with this weight dragging them both down? It was futile to lighten it by lies; their life would never have its old buoyancy. The frost had been there, and the wealth of vines and creepers and clustering roses and blossoms fairer than roses that had entwined them had shed every tiny leaf, lost every blossom, and nothing remained but the tough, naked withes binding them together in an unbreakable tether. What did it avail that she roused the feelings of former days to an artificial life by the warmth of memories, that she put her idol upon its pedestal again, that she called back the light of admiration to her eyes, the words of adoration to her lips, and the flush of happiness to her cheeks! What did it all avail, when he would not take upon himself to be the priest of the idol and so help her to a pious fraud? He! He did not even remember her love. Not one of her words echoed in his ears, not one of all their days was hidden in his soul.

No, dead and cold was the ardent love of their hearts. The fragrance, the glamour, and the tremulous tones — all had been wafted away. There they sat, from force of habit, he with his arm around her waist, she with her head resting on his shoulder, drearily sunk in silence, forgetting each other; she, to remember the glorious hero he had never been; he, to transform her in his dreams to the ideal which he now always saw shining in the sky high above her head. Such was their life together, and the days came and went without bringing any change, and day after day they gazed out over the desert of their lives, and told themselves that it was a desert, that there were no flowers nor any hope of flowers or springs or green palms.

As the autumn advanced, Erik's drinking bouts became more frequent. What was the use, he said to Niels, of sitting at home waiting for ideas that never came, until his thoughts turned to stone in his head? Moreover, he did not get much comfort from Niels's society, he needed people with some grit in them, people of lusty flesh and blood, not a whim-wham of delicate nerves. Niels and Fennimore were therefore left much alone, for Niels came over to Marianelund every day.

The covenant of friendship they had made and the talk they had had on that Sunday afternoon put them at their ease with each other, and, lonely as they both were, they drew closer together in a warm and tender friendship, which soon gained a strong hold over both. It absorbed them so that their thoughts, whether they were together or apart, always turned to this bond, as birds building the same nest look on everything they gather or pass by with the one pleasant goal of making the nest snug and comfortable for each other and themselves.

If Niels came while Erik was away, they nearly always, even on rainy and stormy days, took long walks in the woods behind the garden. They had fallen in love with that forest, and grew fonder of it as they watched

the summer life die out. There were a thousand things to see. First, how
the leaves turned yellow and red and brown, then how they fell off,
whirling on a windy day in yellow swarms, or softly rustling in still air,
single leaf after leaf, down against the stiff boughs and between the
pliant brown twigs. And when the leaves fell from trees and bushes, the
hidden secrets of summer were revealed in nest upon nest. What treasures on the ground and on the branches, dainty seeds and bright-colored
berries, brown nuts, shining acorns and exquisite acorn cups, tassels of
coral on the barberry, polished black berries on the buckthorn, and
scarlet urns on the dogrose. The bare beeches were finely dotted with
prickly beechnuts, and the roan bent under the weight of its red clusters,
acid in fragrance like apple cider. Late brambleberries lay black and
brown among the wet leaves at the wayside; red whortleberries brought
forth their dull crimson fruit for the second time. The ferns turned all
colors as they faded, and the moss was a revelation, not only the deep,
luscious moss in the hollows and on the slopes, but the faint, delicate
growth on the tree trunks, resembling what one might imagine the
cornfields of the elves to be as it sent forth the finest of stalks with dark
brown buds like ears of corn at the tip.

They scoured the forest from end to end, eager to find all its treasures
and marvels. They had divided it between them as children do; the part
on one side of the road was Fennimore's property, and that on the other
side was Niels's, and they would compare their realms and quarrel about
which was the more glorious. Everything there had names – clefts and
hillocks, paths and stiles, ditches and pools; and when they found a
particular magnificent tree, they gave that too a name. In this way they
took complete possession and created a little world of their own which
no one else knew and no one else was at home in, and yet they had no
secret which all the world might not have heard.

As yet they had not.

But love was in their hearts, and was not there, as the crystals are
present in a saturated solution, and yet are not present, not until a
splinter or the merest particle of the right matter is thrown into the
solution, releasing the slumbering atoms as if by magic, and they rush
to meet one another, joining and riveting themselves together according
to unsearchable laws, and in the same instant there is crystal – crystal.

So it was a trifle that made them feel they loved.

There is nothing to tell. It was a day like all other days, when they
were alone together in the sitting room, as they had been a hundred
times before; their conversation was about things of no moment, and
that which happened was outwardly as common and as everydaylike as
possible. It was nothing except that Niels stood looking out of the
window, and Fennimore came over to him and looked out too. That

was all, but it was enough, for in a flash like lightning, the past and present and future were transformed for Niels Lyhne by the consciousness that he loved the woman standing by his side, not as anything bright and sweet and happy and beautiful that would lift him to ecstasy or rapture — such was not the nature of his love — but he loved her as something he could no more do without than the breath of life itself, and he reached out, as a drowning man clutches, and pressed her hand to his heart.

She understood him. With almost a scream, in a voice full of terror and agony, she cried out to him an answer and a confession: "Oh, *yes,* Niels!" and snatched away her hand in the same instant. A moment she stood, pale and shrinking, then sank down with one knee in an upholstered chair, hiding her face against the harsh velvet of the back, and sobbed aloud.

Niels stood a few seconds as though blinded, groping around among the bulb glasses for support. It was only for a very few seconds; then he stepped over to the chair where she was lying, and bent over without touching her, resting one hand on the back of the chair.

"Don't be so unhappy, Fennimore! Look up and let us talk about it. Will you, or will you not? Don't be afraid! Let us bear it together, my own love! Come, try if you can't!

She raised her head slightly and looked up at him. "Oh, God, what shall we do! Isn't it terrible, Niels! Why should such a thing happen to me? And how lovely it all could have been — so happy!" and she sobbed again.

"Should I not have spoken?" he moaned. "Poor Fennimore, would you rather never have known it?"

She raised her head again and caught his hand.

"I wish I knew it and were dead. I wish I were in my grave and knew it, that would be good — oh, so peaceful and good!"

"It is bitter for us both, Fennimore, that the first thing our love brings us should be only misery and tears. Don't you think so?"

"You must not be hard on me, Niels, I can't help it. You can't see it as I do — I am the one that should be strong, because I am the one that is bound. I wish I could take my love and force it back into the most secret depth of my soul and lock it in and be deaf to all its wailing and its prayers, and then tell you to go far, far away; but I can't, I have suffered so much, I can't suffer that too — I can't, Niels. I can't live without you — see, can I? Do you think I can?"

She rose and flung herself on his breast.

"Here I am, and I won't let you go; I won't send you away, while I sit here alone in the old darkness. It is like a bottomless pit of loathing and misery. I won't throw myself into it. I would rather jump into the fjord, Niels. Even if the new life brings other agonies, at least they are new agonies, and haven't the dull sting of the old, and can't stab home like the old, which know my heart so cruelly well. Am I talking wildly? Yes, of course I am, but it is so good to talk to you without any reserve and without having to be careful not to say what I have no right to. For now you have the first right of all! I wish you could take me wholly, so that I could belong to you utterly and not to anyone else at all. I wish you could lift me out of all relations that hedge me in!"

"We must break through them, Fennimore. I will arrange everything as well as possible. Don't be afraid! Some day, before anyone suspects anything, we shall be far away."

"No, no, we mustn't run away, anything but that, anything else rather than have my parents hear their daughter had run away. It is impossible! I will never do it. By God in heaven, Niels, I will never do it."

"Oh, but you must, my dearest, you must. Can't you see all the baseness and ugliness that will rise and close in around us everywhere, if we stay, all the lies and deceptions that will entangle us and drag us down? I won't have you besmirched by all that. I refuse to let it eat into our love like corroding rust."

But she was immovable.

"You don't know what you are condemning us to," he said sadly. "It would be far better to crush under iron heels now instead of being merciful. Believe me, Fennimore, we must let our love be everything to us, the first and only thing in the world, that which must be saved, even at the cost of stabbing where we would rather heal and bringing sorrow where we would rather keep every shadow of sorrow far away. If we don't do that, you will see that the yoke we bend our necks under now will weigh on us and at last force us to our knees, unmercifully, inexorably. – A fight on our knees, you don't know how hard that is! Shall we fight the fight anyway, my dearest, side by side, against everything?"

*F*or the first few days Niels persisted in his attempts to persuade her to flight. Then he began to picture to himself what a blow it would be to Erik if he were to come home one day and find friend and wife gone away together, and by degrees the whole thing took on an unnaturally tragic air of the impossible. He accustomed himself not to think of it, as he did with many other things that he might have wished different, and threw himself with his whole soul into the situation as it was, without any conscious attempts to make it over by dreams or cover its defects with imaginary festoons and garlands. But, oh, how sweet it was to love for once with the love of real life; for now he knew that nothing of what he had imagined to be love was real love, neither the turgid longing of the lonely youth, nor the passionate yearning of the dreamer, nor yet the nervous foreboding of the child. These were currents in the ocean of love, single reflections of its full light, fragments of love as the meteors rushing through space are splinters of a world — for that was love; a world complete in itself, fully rounded, vast, and orderly. It was no medley of confused sensations and moods rushing one upon another! Love was like nature, ever changing, ever renewing; no feeling died and no emotion withered without giving life to the seed of something still more perfect which was imbedded in it. Quietly, sanely, with full, deep breaths — it was good to love so and love with all his soul. The days fell bright and new-coined, down from heaven itself; they no longer followed one upon another as a matter of course like the hackneyed pictures in a peep show. Every one was a revelation. With each day that passed, he felt stronger, greater, and nobler. He had never known such strength and fullness of feeling; there were moments when he seemed to himself titanic, much more than man, so inexhaustible was the well spring of his soul, so broad-winged the tenderness that swelled his heart, so wondrous the sweep of his vision, so infinite the gentleness of his judgments.

This was the beginning of happiness, and they were happy long.

The daily falsehood and deception and the atmosphere of dishonor in which they lived had not yet gained power over them, and could not touch them on those ecstatic heights to which Niels had lifted their relationship and, with it, themselves. For he was not simply a man who seduced his friend's wife — or rather, so he told himself defiantly, he was that man, but he was also the one who saved an innocent woman whom life had wounded, stoned, and defiled, a woman who had lain down to let her soul die. This woman he had given back her confidence in life, her faith in the powers of good; he had lifted her spirit to noble heights, had given her happiness. What, then, was best, the old blameless misery or that which he had won for her? He did not ask, he had made his choice.

He did not quite mean this, if the truth were told. Man often builds for himself theories in which he refuses to dwell. Thoughts often run faster than the sense of right and wrong is willing to follow. Yet the conception was really present in his mind, and it took away some of the cankerous venom inherent in the craftiness, falseness, and duplicity of their lives.

Yet the evil effects were soon noticeable. The poison was working on so many fine nerve filaments that it could not but do harm and cause suffering, and the time was hastened when Erik, shortly after New Year, announced that he had caught an idea — something with a green tunic and a threatening attitude, he told Niels. Did he remember the green in Salvator Rosa's Jonah? Something on that order.

Although Erik's work consisted chiefly in lying on the couch in his studio, smoking shag and reading Marryat, it had at least the effect of keeping him at home for the time being, thereby forcing them to use more caution and necessitating new lies and artifices.

Fennimore's ingenuity in this direction was what brought the first cloud to their heaven. It was scarcely perceptible at first, only a doubt, light as thistledown, flitting through Niels's mind as to whether his love were not nobler than the one he loved. It had not yet taken shape as a thought, it was only a dim foreboding which pointed in that direction, a vague giving way in his mind, a leaning to that side.

Yet it came again and brought others in its wake, thoughts at first vague and indistinct, then clearer and sharper for each time they appeared. It was astonishing with what furious haste these thoughts could undermine, debase, and take away the glamour. Their love was not lessened. On the contrary, it glowed more passionately while it sank, but these handclasps stolen under table covers, these kisses snatched in passages and behind doors, these long looks right under the eyes of him they deceived, took away all the lofty tenor. Happiness no longer stood still above their heads; they had to filch her smiles and her light as best they could, and after a while their wiles and cunning were no longer necessary evils, but amusing triumphs. Deception became their natural element and made them contemptible and petty. There were degrading secrets, too, over which they had hitherto grieved separately, assuming ignorance in each other's eyes, but which they now had to share; for Erik was not bashful, and would often caress his wife in Niels's presence, kiss her, take her on his lap, and embrace her, while Fennimore had neither courage nor dignity sufficient to repel these caresses; the consciousness of her guilt made her uncertain and afraid.

So it sank and went on sinking, that lofty castle of their love, from the pinnacles of which they had gazed so proudly out over the world, and within which they had felt so strong and noble.

Still they were happy among the ruins.

When they walked in the woods now, it was usually on gloomy days, when the fog hung under the dark branches and thickened between the wet trunks, so that none should see how they kissed and embraced, both here and there, and none should hear how their frivolous talk rang with peals of wanton laughter.

The melancholy of eternity, which had exalted their love, was gone; now there was nothing but smiles and jests between them. With feverish haste they snatched greedily at the fleeting seconds of joy, as though they must hurry in their love and had not a lifetime before them.

It brought no change when Erik, after a while, grew tired of his idea and again began his carousing so eagerly that he was rarely at home for forty-eight hours at a stretch. Where they had fallen, there they lay. Once in a great while, perhaps, in lonely hours, they gazed regretfully toward the heights from which they had fallen, or perhaps they only wondered, and thought what a strain it must have been to stay on that level, and felt themselves more snugly housed where they were. There was no change. At least there was no return to the former days, but the flabby uncleanness of living as they did and not running away together became more present in their consciousness and linked them together in a closer and baser union through the common sense of guilt; for neither of them wished any change in things as they were. Nor did they pretend to each other that they did, for there had developed a cynical intimacy between them such as often exists between fellow criminals, and there was nothing in their relations that they shrank from putting into words. With sinister frankness, they called things by their right names and, as they put it to themselves, faced the facts as they were.

*I*n February it had seemed that the winter was over, but then Mother March had come shaking her white mantle with its loose lining, and snowstorm after snowstorm covered the ground with thick layers. Then followed calm weather and hard frost, and the fjord settled under a crust of ice six inches thick, which lay there a long time.

One evening toward the end of the month, Fennimore was sitting alone in her parlor after tea and waiting.

The room was brightly illumined; the piano stood open with candles lit, and the silk shade had been taken from the lamp. The gilded moldings caught the light, and the pictures on the walls seemed to stand out with a kind of vigilance. The hyacinths had been moved from the windows to the writing table, where they made a mass of delicate colors, filling the air with a penetrating fragrance that seemed cool in its purity. The fire in the stove burned with a pleasant subdued crackle.

Fennimore was walking up and down the room almost as if she were balancing on a dark red stripe in the carpet. She wore a somewhat old-fashioned black silk dress with a heavily embroidered edge that weighed it down and trailed, first on one side, then on the other, with every step she took.

She was humming to herself and holding with both hands a string of large pale yellow amber beads that hung from her neck. Whenever she wavered on the red stripe, she would stop humming, but still grasped the necklace. Perhaps she was making an omen for herself: if she could walk a certain number of times up and down without getting off the red stripe and without letting go with her hands, Niels would come.

He had been there in the morning, when Erik went away, and had stayed till late in the afternoon, but he had promised to come again as soon as the moon was up and it was light enough to see the holes in the ice on the fjord.

Fennimore had obtained her omen, whatever it was, and stepped over to the window.

It looked as if there would not be any moon tonight; the sky was very black, and the darkness must be more intense out there on the grey-blue fjord than on land where the snow lay. Perhaps it was best that he did not attempt it. She sat down at the piano with a sigh of resignation, then got up again to look at the clock. She came back and resolutely propped up a big book of music before her, but did not play, merely turning the leaves absentmindedly, lost in her own thoughts.

Suppose, after all, that he was standing on the opposite shore this very moment, fastening on his skates. He could be here in an instant! She saw him plainly, a little bit out of breath after skating, and blinking with his eyes against the light on coming from the darkness outside. He would bring a breath of cold air, and his beard would be full of tiny little bright drops. Then he would say — what would he say?

She smiled and glanced down at herself.

And still the moon did not appear.

She went over to the window again and stood gazing out, till the darkness seemed to be filled before her eyes with tiny white sparks and rainbow-colored rings. But they were only a vague glimmer. She wished they would be transformed into fireworks out there, rockets shooting up in long, long curves and then turning to tiny snakes that bored their way into the sky and died in a flicker; or into a great, huge pale ball that hung tremulous in the sky and slowly sank down in a rain of myriad-colored stars. Look! Look! Soft and rounded like a curtsy, like a golden rain that curtsied. — Farewell! Farewell! There went the last one: — Oh, if he would only come! She did not want to play — and at that she turned to the piano, struck an octave harshly, and held the keys down till the tones had quite died away, then did the same again, and again, and yet again. She did not want to play, did not want to. — She would rather dance! For a moment she closed her eyes, and in imagination she felt herself whirling through a vast hall of red and white and gold. How delicious it would be to have danced and to be hot and tired and drink champagne! Suddenly she remembered how she and a school friend had concocted champagne from soda water and eau de cologne, and how sick it had made them when they drank it.

She straightened herself and walked across the room, instinctively smoothing her dress as after a dance.

"And now let us be sensible!" she said, took her embroidery and settled herself in a large armchair near the lamp.

Yet she did not work; her hands sank down into her lap, and soon she snuggled down into the chair with little lazy movements, fitting herself into its curves, her face resting on her hand, her dress wrapped around her feet.

She wondered curiously whether other wives were like her, whether they had made a mistake and been unhappy and then had loved someone else. She passed in review the ladies at home in Fjordby, one by one. Then she thought of Mrs. Boye. Niels had told her about Mrs. Boye, and she had always been a tantalizing riddle to her — this woman whom she hated and felt humiliated by.

Erik, too, had once told her that he had been madly in love with Mrs. Boye.

Ah, if one could know everything about her!

She laughed at the thought of Mrs. Boye's new husband.

All the time, while her thoughts were thus engaged, she was longing and listening for Niels, and imagined him coming, always coming out there on the ice. She little guessed that for the last two hours a tiny black dot had been working its way over the snowy meadows with a message for her very different from the one she was expecting from across the fjord. It was only a man in homespun and greased boots, and now he tapped on the kitchen window, frightening the maid.

It was a letter, Trine said when she came in to her mistress. Fennimore took it. It was a telegram. Quietly she gave the maid the receipt and dismissed her; she was not in the least alarmed, for Erik of late had often telegraphed that he would bring one or two guests home with him the following day.

Then she read.

Suddenly she turned white and darted wildly from her seat out into the middle of the room, staring at the door with expectant terror.

She would not let it come into the house, did not dare to, and with one bound she threw herself against the door, pressing her shoulder against it, and turned the key till it cut her hand. But it would not turn, no matter how hard she tried. Her hand dropped. Then she remembered that the thing was not here at all — it was far away from her in a strange house.

She began to shake, her knees would no longer support her, and she slid along the door to the floor.

Erik was dead. The horses had run away, had overturned the carriage at a street corner, and hurled Erik with his head against the wall. His skull had been fractured, and now he lay dead at Aalborg. That was the way it had happened, and most of this story was told in the telegram. No one had been with him in the carriage except the white-necked tutor known as the Arab. It was he who had telegraphed.

She crouched on the floor moaning feebly, both palms spread out on the carpet, her eyes staring with a fixed, empty look, as she swayed helplessly to and fro.

Only a moment ago everything had been light and fragrance around her, and, however much she tried, she could not instantly put all this out of her consciousness to admit the inky black night of grief and remorse. It was not her fault that her mind was still haunted by fitful, dazzling gleams of love's happiness and love's pleasure; that intense, foolish desires would force their way out of the whirl, seeking the bliss of forgetfulness, or trying to stop with a frenzied wrench the revolving wheel of fortune.

But it soon passed.

In black swarms, from everywhere, dark thoughts came flying like ravens, lured by the corpse of her happiness, and hacked it beak by beak, even while the warmth of life still lingered in it. They tore and slashed and made it hideous and unrecognizable, until the whole thing was nothing but a carrion of loathing and horror.

She rose and walked about, supporting herself by chairs and tables like one who is ill. Desperately she looked around for some cobweb of help, if it were only a comforting glance, a sympathetic pat on the hand, but her eyes met nothing but the glaring family portraits, all the strangers who had been witnesses of her fall and her crime — sleepy old gentlemen, prim-mouthed matrons, and their ever-present gnome child, the girl with the great round eyes and bulging forehead. It had acquired memories enough at last, this strange furniture, the table over there, and that chair, the footstool with the black poodle dog, and the portiere like a dressing gown, — she had saturated them all with memories, adulterous memories, which they now spewed out and flung after her. Oh, it was terrible to be locked in with all these specters of crime and with herself. She shuddered at herself; she pointed accusing fingers at herself, at this dishonored Fennimore who crouched at her feet, she pulled her dress away from between her imploring hands.

Mercy? No, there was no mercy! How could there be mercy before those dead eyes in the strange town, those eyes which had become seeing, now that they were glazed in death, and saw how she had thrown his honor in the mud, lied at his lips, been faithless at his heart.

She could feel those dead eyes riveted on her; she did not know whence they came, but they followed her, gliding down her body like two ice-cold rays. As she looked down, while every thread of the carpet, every stitch in the footstools, seemed unnaturally clear in the strong sharp light, she felt something walking about her with the footsteps of dead men, felt it brushing against her dress so distinctly that she screamed with terror, and darted to one side. But it came in front of her like hands and yet not like hands, something that clutched at her slowly, clutched derisively and triumphantly at her heart, that marvel of treachery, that yellow pearl of deceit! And she retreated till she backed up against the table, but it was still there, and her bosom gave no protection against it; it clutched through her skin and flesh . . . She almost died of terror, as she stood there, helplessly bending back over the table, while every nerve contracted with fear and her eyes stared as if they were being murdered in their sockets.

Then that passed.

She looked around with a haunted look, then sank down on her knees and prayed a long time. She repented and confessed, wildly and unrestrainedly, in growing passion, with the same fanatic self-loathing that drives the nun to scourge her naked body. She sought fervently after the most groveling expressions, intoxicating herself with self-abasement and with a humility that thirsted for degradation.

At last she rose. Her bosom heaved violently, and there was a faint light in the pale cheeks, which seemed to have grown fuller during her prayer.

She looked around the room as if she were taking a silent vow. Then she went into the adjoining room, closed the door after her, stood still a moment as though to accustom herself to the darkness, groped her way to the door which opened on the glass enclosed veranda, and went out.

It was lighter there. The moon had risen, and shone through the close-packed frozen crystals on the glass; the light came yellowish through the panes, blue and red through the squares of colored glass that framed them.

She melted a hole in the ice with her hand and carefully wiped away the moisture with her handkerchief.

As yet there was no one in sight out on the fjord.

She began to walk up and down in her glass cage. There was no furniture out there except a settee of cane and bent wood, covered with withered ivy leaves from the vines overhead. Every time she passed it, the leaves rustled faintly with the stirring of the air, and now and then her dress caught a leaf on the floor, drawing it along with a scratching sound over the boards.

Back and forth she walked on her dreary watch, her arms folded over her breast, hardening herself against the cold.

He came.

She opened the door with a quick wrench, and stepped out into the frozen snow in her thin shoes. She had no pity on herself, she could have gone barefooted to that meeting.

Niels had slowed up at the sight of the black figure against the snow and was skating toward land with hesitating, tentative strokes.

That stealthy figure seemed to burn into her eyes. Every familiar movement and feature struck her as a shameless insult, as a boast of degrading secrets. She shook with hatred; her heart swelled with curses, and she could scarcely control her anger.

"It is I!" she cried to him jeeringly, "the harlot, Fennimore!"

"But for God's sake, sweetheart?" he asked, astonished, as he came within a few feet of her.

"Erik is dead."

"Dead! When?" He had to step out into the snow with his skates to keep from falling. "Oh, but tell me!" Eagerly he took a step nearer.

They were now standing close together, and she had to restrain herself from striking that pale, distorted face with her clenched fist.

"I will tell you, never fear," she cried. "He is dead, as I said. He had a runaway in Aalborg and got his head crushed, while we were deceiving him here."

"It is terrible!" Niels moaned, pressing his hands to his temples. "Who could have dreamed — Oh, I wish we had been faithful to him, Fennimore! Erik, poor Erik! — I wish I were in his place!" He sobbed aloud, writhing with pain.

"I hate you, Niels Lyhne!"

"Oh, what does it matter about us?" Niels groaned; "if we could only get him back! Poor Fennimore!" he said with a change of feeling. "Never mind me. You hate me, you say? You may well hate me." He rose suddenly. "Let us go in," he said. "I don't know what I am saying. Who was it that telegraphed, did you say?"

"In!" Fennimore screamed, infuriated by his failure to notice her hostility. "In there! Never shall you set your craven, despicable foot inside that house again. How dare you think of it, you wretch, you false creature, who came sneaking in here and stole your friend's honor, because it was too poorly hidden! What, did you not steal it under his very eyes, because he thought you were honest, you house thief!"

"Hush, hush, are you mad? What is the matter with you! What sort of language are you using?" He had caught her arm firmly, drawing her to him, and looked straight into her face in amazement. "You must try to come to your senses, child," he said in a gentler tone. "You can't mend matters by slinging ugly words."

She wrenched her arm away with such force that he staggered and almost lost his uncertain foothold.

"Can't you hear that I hate you!" she screamed shrilly. "And isn't there so much of a decent man's brain left in you that you can understand it! How blind I must have been when I loved you, you patched together with lies, when I had him at my side, who was ten thousand times better than you. I shall hate and despise you to the end of my life. Before you came, I was honest, I had never done anything wicked; but then you came with your poetry and your rubbish and dragged me down with your lies, into the mud with you. What have I done to you that you could not leave me alone — I who should have been sacred to you above all others! Now I have to live day after day with this shameful blot on my soul, and I shall never meet anyone so base but that I know myself to be baser. All the memories of my girlhood you have poisoned. What have I to look back on that is clean and good now! You have tainted everything. It is not only he that is dead, everything bright and good that has been between us is dead, too, and rotten. Oh, God help me, is it fair that I can't get any revenge on you after all you have done? Make me honest again, Niels Lyhne, make me pure and good again! No, no — but it ought to be possible to torture you into undoing the wrong you have done. Can you undo it with lies? Don't stand there and crouch under your own helplessness. I want to see you suffer, here before my eyes, and writhe in pain and despair and be miserable. Let him be miserable, God, do not let him steal my revenge too! Go, you wretch, go! I cast you off, but be sure that I drag you with me through all the agonies my hate can call down over you."

She had stretched out her arms menacingly. Now she turned and went in, and the veranda door rattled softly, as she closed it.

Niels stood looking after her in amazement, almost with disbelief. That pale, vengeful face seemed to be still there before him, so strangely ignoble and coarse, all its delicate beauty of contour gone, as if a rough, barbarous hand had plowed up all its lines.

He stumbled cautiously down to the ice and began to skate slowly toward the mouth of the fjord, with the moonlight in front of him and the wind in his back. Gradually he increased his speed, as his thoughts took his attention from the surroundings, till the ice splinters flew from the runners of his skates and rattled on the smooth surface, blown along with him by the rising frost wind.

So that was the end! So that was the way he had saved this woman's soul and lifted it and given it happiness! It was certainly beautiful, his relation to the dead friend, his childhood friend, for whom he would have sacrificed his future, his life, his all! He with his sacrificing and his saving! Let heaven and earth behold in him a man who preserved his life on the heights of honor without spot or blemish in order not to cast a shadow over the Idea he served and was called to promulgate.

No doubt that was another of his boastful fancies that his paltry little life could put spots on the sun of the Idea. Good God, he was always taking these high and mighty views of himself, it was bred in his bone. If he could not be anything better, he must at least be a Judas and call himself Iscariot in grandiose gloom. That sounded like something. Was he forever going to put on airs as if he were a responsible minister to the Idea, a member of its privy council, getting everything concerning humanity at first hand! Would he never learn to do his duty in barrack service for the Idea with all simplicity as a private of a very subordinate class?

There were red fires out on the ice, and he skated so near them that a gigantic shadow shot out for a moment from his feet, turned forward, and disappeared again.

He thought of Erik and of what kind of friend he had been to Erik. He! His childhood memories wrung their hands over him; his youthful dreams covered their heads and wept over him; his whole past stared after him with a long look full of reproach. He had betrayed it all for a love as small and mean as himself. There *had* been exaltation in this love, but he had betrayed that too.

Whither could he flee to escape these attempts that always ended in the ditch? All his life had been nothing else, and it would never be anything else in the future; he knew that and felt it with such certainty that he sickened at the thought of all this futile endeavor, and he wished with all his soul that he could run away and escape this meaningless fate. If only the ice would break under him now as he skated, and all would be over with a gasp and a spasm in the cold water!

He stopped, exhausted, and looked back. The moon had gone down, and the fjord stretched long and dark between the white hills on either side. Then he turned and worked his way back against the wind. It was very strong now, and he was tired. He skated closer to the shore to get the shelter of the hills, but, as he struggled thus, he came on a hole in the ice made by the winds sweeping down from the hills, and he felt the thin, elastic crust give way under him with a crackling sound.

Ah, he breathed more easily, in spite of all, when he set foot on the firm ice again! Under the stimulus of fear, his exhaustion had almost left him, and he skated on vigorously.

*W*hile he was struggling out there, Fennimore sat in the lighted room, baffled and miserable. She felt herself cheated out of her revenge. She hardly knew what she had expected, but it was something entirely different; she had had a vision of something mighty and majestic, something of swords and red flames, or — not that, but something that would sweep her along and lift her to a throne, but instead it had all turned out so small and paltry, and she had felt more like a common scold than like one who utters curses. . . .

After all, she had learned something from Niels.

*E*arly in the morning of the following day, while Niels, overcome with exhaustion, was still asleep, she left the house.

Chapter XII

*F*or the better part of two years Niels Lyhne had roamed about on the Continent. He was very lonely, without kith or kin or any close friend of his heart. Yet there was another and greater loneliness that encompassed him; for however desolate and forsaken a man may feel when he has no single spot on all this vast earth to which his affections can cling, which he can bless when the heart *will* overflow and yearn for when longing *will* spread its wings, there is no existence so lonely that he is utterly alone if he can only see the fixed bright star of a life goal shining overhead. But Niels Lyhne had no star. He did not know what to do with himself and his gifts. It was all very well to have talent if he could only have used it, but he went about like a painter without hands. How he envied the people, great and small, who always, whenever they reached out into life, found a handle to lay hold of; for he could never find any handle. It seemed as though he could do nothing but sing over again the old romantic songs, and in truth he had so far done nothing else. His talent was like something apart in him, a quiet Pompeii, or a harp that had to be taken out of its corner. It was not all-pervading, did not run down the street with him or tingle in his fingertips — not in the least. His talent had no grip on him. Sometimes it seemed to him that he had been born half a century too late, sometimes that he had come altogether too early. His talent was rooted in something of the past; it could not draw nourishment from his opinions, his convictions, and his sympathies, could not absorb them and give them form. The two elements seemed always to be gliding apart like water and oil, which can be shaken together, but can never mix, never become one.

Gradually, as he began to realize this, he sank Into a boundless dejection and grew inclined to take an ironic, suspicious view of himself and his whole past. There must be something wrong with him, he told himself, something incurably wrong in the very marrow of his being; for surely a man could fuse the varying elements in his own nature — that he firmly believed.

This was the state of his mind when he settled down, in the month of September, toward the end of the second year of his exile, on the shores of Lake Garda, in the little town of Biva.

Not long afterward, the region was hedged about by difficulties that put a stop to traveling and kept all strangers away. Cholera had broken out round about Venice and down south in Descensano and in the north by the Trentino. Under these circumstances, Riva was not lively, for the hotels had been emptied at the first rumor, and tourists bound for Italy took another route.

Naturally, the few people who remained drew all the more closely together.

The most remarkable person among them was a famous opera singer, whose real name was Madame Odero. Her stage name was far more celebrated. She and her companion, Niels, and a deaf doctor from Vienna were the only guests at the Golden Sun, the leading hotel in town.

Niels felt very much attracted to her, and she yielded to that warmth of manner in him which is often a characteristic of people who are at strife with themselves and therefore feel the need of establishing their relations with others on a safe basis.

Madame Odero had lived there for nearly seven months, trying to recover, by complete rest, from the aftereffects of a throat trouble that had threatened her voice. Her physician had told her to abstain for a year from singing and, in order to avoid temptation, from all music. Not until the year was over would he allow her to attempt to sing, and then, if no weariness followed, she might consider herself cured.

Niels acquired a kind of civilizing influence over Madame Odero, who was a fiery, passionate nature with no fine shades. It had been a terrible sentence to her when she was condemned to live a whole year without applause and adoration, and at first she had been in despair, gazing horror-stricken at the twelve months stretching before her as upon a deep, black grave into which she was being thrust; but everybody seemed to think it was unavoidable, and one fine morning she suddenly fled to Riva. It would have been quite possible for her to have lived in a livelier and more frequented place, but that was the very thing she sought to avoid. She felt ashamed, as though she had been marked with an outward visible blemish, imagining that people pitied her because of this infirmity, and that they discussed her among themselves. Therefore she had shunned all society in her new abode and had lived almost entirely in her rooms, where she sometimes took revenge on the doors when her voluntary confinement became unbearable.

Now that everybody had left, she appeared again and learned to know Niels Lyhne, for she was not at all afraid of people individually.

No one needed to be long in Madame Odero's presence before finding out whether she liked him or not, for she showed it with sufficient plainness. What she gave Niels Lyhne to see was very encouraging, and they had not been alone for many days in the magnificent hotel garden with its pomegranates and myrtles, with its arbors of blossoming nerias and its marvelous view, before they were on very friendly terms.

They were not at all in love with each other, or if they were, it was not very serious. It was one of the vague, pleasant intimacies that will sometimes grow up between men and women who are past the time of early youth when nature flames up and yearns toward an unknown bliss. It is a kind of waning summer, in which people promenade decorously side by side, gather themselves into graceful nosegays, each caressing himself with the other's hand and admiring himself with the other's eyes. They take out all their store of pretty secrets, all the exquisite useless trifles people accumulate like bric-à-brac of the soul, pass them from hand to hand, turn them round and hold them up, seeking the most artistic light effect, comparing and analyzing.

It is, of course, only when life passes in a leisurely way that such Sunday friendships are possible, and here by the quiet lake these two had plenty of time. Niels had made a beginning by draping Madame Odero in a becoming robe of melancholy. At first, she was several times on the point of tearing the whole thing off and revealing herself as the barbarian she was, but when she found that she could wear the drapery with patrician effect, she took her melancholy as a role, and not only stopped slamming the doors, but sought out the moods and emotions in herself that might suit her new pose. It was astonishing how she came to realize that she had actually known herself very little in the past. Her life had, in fact, been too eventful and exciting to give her time for exploring herself, and besides she was only now approaching the age when women who have lived much in the world and seen much commence to collect their memories, to look back at themselves and assemble a past.

From this beginning, their intimacy developed quickly and definitely until they had become quite indispensable to each other. Each led only a half-hearted existence without the other.

Then it happened one morning, as Niels was starting out for a sail, that he heard Madame Odero singing in the garden. His first impulse was to turn back and scold her, but before he could make up his mind, the boat had carried him out of hearing; the wind tempted him to a trip to Limone, and he meant to be back by midday. So he sailed on.

Madame Odero had descended into the garden earlier than usual. The fresh fragrance that filled the air, the round waves rising and sinking clear and bright as glass beneath the garden wall, and all this glory of color everywhere — blue lake and sun-scorched mountains, white sails flitting across the lake and red flowers arching over her head — all this and with it a dream she could not forget, which went on throbbing against her heart . . . She could not be silent, she had to be a part of all this life.

Therefore she sang.

Fuller and fuller rose the exultant notes of her voice. She was intoxicated with its beauty, she trembled in a voluptuous sense of its power; and she went on, she could not stop, for she was borne blissfully along on wonderful dreams of coming triumphs.

No weariness followed. She could leave, leave at once, shake off the nothingness of the past months, come out of her hiding and live!

By midday everything was ready for her departure.

Then, just as the carriages drove up to the door, she remembered Niels Lyhne. She dived down into her pocket for a paltry little notebook, and scribbled it full of farewells to Niels, for the pages were so small that each could hold only three or four words. This she enclosed in an envelope for him and departed.

When Niels came back in the late afternoon, after being detained by the sanitary police in Limone, she had long since reached Mori and taken the train.

He was not surprised, only sorry, and not at all angry. He could even smile resignedly at this new hostile thrust of fate. But in the evening, when he sat in the empty moonlit garden telling the innkeeper's little boy the story about the princess who found her wings again and flew away from her lover back to the land of fairies, he was seized with an intolerable longing for Lonborggaard. He yearned to feel something closing around him like a home and holding him fast, no matter how. He could not bear the indifference of life any longer, could not endure being cast off and thrown back on himself again and again. No home on earth, no God in heaven, no goal out there in the future! He would at least have a home. He would make it his own by loving everything there, big and little, every rock, every tree, the animate and the inanimate; he would portion out his heart to it all so that it could never cast him off anymore.

Chapter XIII

*F*or about a year, Niels Lyhne had lived at Lönborggaard, managing the farm as well as he knew how and as much as his old steward would let him. He had taken down his shield, blotted out his 'scutcheon, and resigned. Humanity would have to get along without him; he had learned to know the joy found in purely physical labor, in seeing the pile growing under his hand, in being able to get through with what he was doing so that he really *was* through, in knowing that when he went away tired the strength that he had used up lay behind him in his work, and the work would stand and not be eaten up by doubt in the night or dispersed by the breath of criticism on the morning after. There were no Sisyphus stones in agriculture.

What joy it was, too, when he had worked till he was tired, to go to bed and gather strength in sleep and to spend it again, as regularly as day and night followed one upon the other, never hindered by the caprices of his brain, never having to handle himself gingerly like a tuned guitar with loose pegs.

He was really happy in a quiet way, and often he would sit, as his father had sat, on a stile or a boundary stone, staring out over the golden wheat or the top-heavy oats, in a strange, vegetative trance.

As yet he had not begun to seek the society of the neighboring families, except Councilor Skinnerup's in Varde, whom he visited quite frequently.

The Skinnerups had come to town while his father was still living, and as the Councilor was an old university friend of Lyhne's, the two families had seen much of each other. Skinnerup, a mild, baldheaded man with sharp features and kind eyes, was now a widower, but his house was more than filled by his four daughters, the eldest seventeen, the youngest twelve years old.

The Councilor had read much, and Niels enjoyed a chat with him on various esthetic subjects, for though he had learned to use his hands, that, of course, did not turn him into a country bumpkin all at once. He was rather amused sometimes at the almost absurd care he had to exercise whenever the conversation turned to a comparison between Danish and foreign literature and, in fact, whenever Denmark was measured against something not Danish. Caution was absolutely necessary, however, for the mild-mannered Councilor was one of the fierce patriots, occasionally met with in those days, who might grudgingly admit that Denmark was not the greatest of the world powers, but when so much was said would not subscribe to a jot or a tittle more that might place his country or anything pertaining to it anywhere but in the lead.

These conversations had another charm, which Niels felt at first vaguely and without consciously thinking of it, in the look of delighted admiration with which seventeen-year-old Gerda's eyes followed him as he spoke. She always managed to be present when he came, and would listen so eagerly that he often saw her flushing with rapture when he said something that seemed to her especially beautiful.

The truth was, he had unwittingly become this young lady's ideal, at first chiefly because he often rode into town wearing a grey mantle of a very foreign and romantic cut, then because he always said Milano instead of Milan, and finally because he was alone in the world and had rather a sad countenance. There were certainly a great many ways in which he differed from the rest of the people in Varde and in Ringkjöbing too.

*O*n a hot summer day, Niels came through the narrow street behind the Councilor's garden. The sun was pouring down over the brick-red little houses, and the ships lying out on the sound had mats hung over their sides to prevent the tar from melting and oozing out of the seams. Round about him everything was open to admit a coolness which did not exist. Within the open doors, the children were reading their lessons aloud, and the hum of their voices mingled with that of the bees in the garden, while a flock of sparrows hopped silently from tree to tree, all flying up together and coming down together.

Niels entered a little house right behind the garden, and while the woman went to bring her husband from the neighbor's, he was left alone in a spotless little room smelling of gillyflowers and freshly ironed linen.

When he had examined the pictures on the walls, the two dogs on the dresser, and the sea shells on the lid of the work box, he stepped over to the open window, whence he heard the sound of Gerda's voice, and there were the four Skinnerup girls on the Councilor's bleaching green only a few steps away.

The balsamines and other flowers in the window hid him, and he prepared himself both to listen and to look.

It was clear that a quarrel was going on, and the three younger sisters were making common cause against Gerda. All carried whips of lemon-yellow withes. The youngest had formed three or four of them into rings wound around with red bark, and had put them on her head like a turban.

It was she who was speaking.

"She says he looks like Themistocles on the stove in the study," she remarked to her fellow conspirators, and turned up her eyes with a rapt expression.

"Oh, pshaw," said the middle one, a saucy little lady who had just been confirmed that spring; "do you suppose Themistocles was round-shouldered?" She imitated Niels Lyhne's slight stoop. "Themistocles! Not much!"

"There is something so manly in his look; he is a real man!" quoted the twelve-year-old.

"He!" came the voice of the middle one again. "Why, he goes and pours eau de cologne on himself. The other day his gloves were lying there and just simply reeking with millefleur."

"*Every* perfection!" breathed the twelve-year-old in ecstasy, and staggered back as though overcome with emotion.

They addressed all these remarks to each other and pretended not to notice Gerda, who stood at a little distance, blushing furiously, as she poked the ground with her yellow stick. Suddenly she lifted her head.

"You're a pair of naughty hussies," she said, "to talk like that about someone who is too good to look at you."

"And yet you know he is *only* a mortal," remonstrated the eldest of the three mildly, as if to make peace.

"No, he is *nothing* of the kind."

"And *surely* he has his faults," continued the sister, pretending not to hear what Gerda said.

"No!"

"But, my dear Gerda, you *know* he never goes to church."

"What should he go there for? He knows *ever* so much more than the pastor."

"Yes, but unfortunately he doesn't believe in any God *at all*, Gerda."

"Well, you can be mighty sure, my dear, that if he doesn't, he has *excellent* reasons for it."

"Why, Gerda, how can you say such a thing!"

"You'd almost think —" broke in the middle one.

"What would you almost think?" snapped Gerda.

"Nothing, nothing at all. Please don't bite me!" replied the sister with a sudden air of great meekness.

"Now will you tell me this minute what you meant!"

"No, no, no, no, no; I guess I've a right to hold my tongue if I want to."

She walked off together with the twelve-year-old, each with her arm around the other's shoulder in sisterly concord. The eldest followed them, strutting with indignation.

Gerda, left alone, stood looking defiantly straight ahead, while she cut the air with her yellow stick.

There was a moment of silence, and then the thin voice of the twelve-year-old floated up from the other end of the garden, singing:

"You ask me, my lad,
  What I want with the withered flower —"

Niels understood their teasing perfectly, for he had recently made Gerda a present of a book with a dried vine leaf from the garden in Verona which contains Juliet's grave. He could hardly keep from laughing; but just then the woman returned with her husband, whom she had at last found, and Niels had to give the order for the carpenter work he had come to see about.

From that day Niels observed Gerda more closely, and every time he saw her he felt more keenly how sweet and fine she was. As time went on, his thoughts turned more and more frequently to this confiding little girl.

She was very lovely, with the tender, appealing beauty that almost brings tears to the eyes. Her figure, in its early ripening, retained something of the child's round-ness, which gave an air of innocence to her luxuriant womanhood. The small, softly molded hands were losing the rosy color of adolescence, and were without any of the restless, nervous curiosity often seen at that age. She had a strong little neck, cheeks that were rounded with a large, full line, and a low, dreamy little woman's forehead, where great thoughts were strangers and almost seemed to hurt when they came, bringing a frown to the thick brows. And her eyes — how deep and blue they lay there, but deep only as a lake where one can see the bottom; and in the soft corners the smile brooded happily under lids that were lifted in slow surprise. This was the way she looked, little Gerda, white and pink and blonde, with all her short, bright hair demurely gathered into a knot.

They had many a talk, Niels and Gerda, and he fell more and more in love with her. Open and frank and chivalrous was his regard, until a certain day there came a change in the air about them, a gleam of that which is too imponderable to be called sensuousness and yet is of the senses, that which impels the hand and mouth and eyes to reach out for what the heart cannot get close enough to its own heart. And another day, not long after, Niels went to Gerda's father, because Gerda was so young, and because he was so sure of her love. And her father said yes, and Gerda said yes. In the spring they were married.

*I*t seemed to Niels Lyhne that existence had grown wonderfully clear and uncomplicated, that life was simple to live and happiness as near and easy to win as the air he drew in with his breath.

He loved her, the young wife he had won, with all the delicacy of thought and feeling, with all the large, deep tenderness of a man who knows the tendency of love to sink and believe in the power of love to rise. How he guarded this young soul which bent toward him with infinite trust and pressed up against him in caressing faith, in implicit reliance that he would do her nothing but good, as the ewe lamb in the parable must have felt toward its shepherd when it ate from his hand and drank of his cup! He had no heart to take her God away from her or to banish all those white hosts of angels that fly singing through the heavens all day and come to earth at eventide and spread their wings from bed to bed, watching faithfully and filling the darkness of night with a protection wall of invisible light. He shrank from allowing his own heavier, imageless view of life to come between her and the soft blue of the heavens and make her feel uneasy and forsaken.

But she would have it otherwise. She wanted to share everything with him; there must be no place in heaven or on earth where their ways were parted. Say what he would to hold her back, she met it all, if not with the words of the Moabite woman, yet with the same obstinate thought that lay in the words — thy people shall be my people, and thy God my God.

Then he began to teach her in earnest. He explained to her that all gods were the work of men and, like everything else made by men, could not endure eternally, but must pass away, generation after generation of gods — because humanity is everlastingly developing and growing beyond its own ideals. A god on whom the noblest and greatest of men could not lavish the richest gifts of their spirit, a god that did not take his light from men, but had to give light by virtue of his own being, a god that was not developing but stiffened in the historic plaster of dogmas, was no longer a god, but an idol. Therefore Judaism was right against Baal and Astarte, and Christianity was right against Judaism, for an idol is nothing in the world. Humanity had gone on from god to god, and therefore Christ could say, on the one hand, looking toward the old God, that He had not come to destroy the law, but to fulfill it, while on the other hand He could point beyond Himself to a yet higher ideal with those mystical words about the sin that shall not be forgiven, the sin against the Holy Ghost.

He went on to teach her how the belief in a personal God who guides everything for the best and who punishes and rewards beyond the grave is a running away from the harsh realities of life, an impotent attempt to take the sting from its arbitrariness. He showed her that it must blunt compassion and make people less ready to exert all their powers in relieving misery, since they could soothe themselves with the thought that suffering in this brief earthly life paved the way for the sufferer to an eternity of glory and joy.

He laid stress on the strength and self-reliance mankind would gain when men had learned faith in themselves, and when the individual strove to bring his life into harmony with what seemed to him, in his best moments, the highest that dwelt in him, instead of seeking it outside of himself in a controlling deity. He made his faith as beautiful and blessed as he could, but he did not conceal from her how crushingly sad and comfortless the truth of atheism would seem in the hour of sorrow compared to the old fair, happy dream of a Heavenly Father who guides and rules. Yet she was brave. It is true, many of his doctrines, and often those he had least expected to affect her, would shake her to the innermost depths of her soul, but her faith knew no bounds; her love carried her with him away from all heavens, and she believed because she loved. Then, after a while, when the new ideas had grown familiar and homelike, she became intolerant in the highest degree and fanatical, as young disciples always are who love their master intensely. Niels often reproached her for it, but that was the one thing she could never understand — that when their belief was true, that of others should not be horrible and reprehensible.

For three years they lived happily together, and much of this happiness shone from a baby face, the face of a little boy who had been born to them in the second year of their marriage.

Happiness usually makes people good, and Niels strove earnestly to make their lives so beautiful, noble, and useful that there should never be any pause in the growth of their souls toward the human ideal in which they both believed. But he no longer thought of carrying the standard of his ideal out into the world; he was content to follow it. Once in a while, he would take out some of his old attempts, and then he would always wonder if it was really he who had written these pretty, artistic tilings. His own verses invariably brought tears to his eyes, but he would not for anything in the world have changed places with the poor fellow who wrote them.

Suddenly, in the spring, Gerda fell ill and could not recover.

Early one morning — it was the last — Niels was sitting up with her. The sun was about to rise and cast a red glow on the white shade curtains, although the light coming in on either side was still blue, making blue shadows in the folds of the white bedspread and under Gerda's pale, thin hands, which lay clasped before her on the sheet. Her cap had slipped off, and, as her head lay far back on the pillow, her features, sharpened and refined by suffering, had an unfamiliar and strangely distinguished air. She moved her lips as if to moisten them, and Niels reached for a glass holding a dark red liquid, but she shook her head faintly. Then suddenly she turned her face to him and gazed anxiously into his mournful countenance. As she looked at the deep sorrow his face revealed and the despair it could not hide, her uneasy foreboding gradually changed to a terrible certainty.

She struggled to rise, but could not.

Niels bent over her quickly, and she caught his hand.

"Is it death?" she asked, lowering her weak voice as if she could not bear to speak the words.

He could only look at her, while his breath came in a deep, moaning sigh.

Gerda clutched his hand and threw herself over to him in her fear. " I don't dare to," she said.

He slid down on his knees by the bed and put his arm under the pillow so that he almost held her to his breast. He could hardly see her for the tears that blinded him as they coursed down his cheeks one after another, and he lifted her hand with a corner of the sheet to his eyes. Then he mastered his voice. "Tell me everything, Gerda dear; never mind me. Would you like to have the pastor come?" He could hardly believe it was that, and there was a note of doubt in his voice.

She did not answer, but closed her eyes and drew her head back a little as if to be alone with her thoughts.

A few minutes passed. The soft, long-drawn whistle of a blackbird sounded underneath the windows; then another whistle and another; a whole series of flutelike notes shot through the silence of the room.

Then she looked up again. "If you were with me," she said, and she leaned more heavily on the pillow that he supported. There was a caress in her movement, and he felt it. "If you were with me! But alone!"

She drew his hand toward her feebly and dropped it again. "I don't dare to." Her eyes were full of fear. "You must fetch him, Niels, I don't dare to come up there alone like this. We had never thought that I should die first; it was always you who went before. Yes, I know-but suppose, after all, we have been mistaken; we *might* have been mistaken, Niels, mightn't we? You don't think so, but it would be strange if *everybody* should be wrong, and if there wasn't anything at all — those big churches and the bells when they bury people — I have always been so fond of the bells." She lay quite still as if she were listening for them and could hear them.

"It is impossible, Niels, that it should all be over, when we die. You don't feel it, you who are well, you think it must kill us quite, because we are so weak, and everything seems to pass away, but it is only the world outside, within us there is as much soul as before. It is there, Niels; I have it all within me, everything that has been given me, the same infinite world, but more quiet, more alone with myself, as when you close your eyes. It is just like a candle, Niels, that is being carried away from you into the darkness, into the darkness, and it seems to you fainter and fainter and fainter, and you can't see it, but still it is shining over there where it is — far away. I always thought I should live to be such an old, old woman, and that I should stay here with you all, and now they won't let me, they are taking me away from the house and home and making me go all alone. I am afraid, Niels, that where I am going it is God who rules, and He cares nothing for our cleverness here on earth. He wants His own way and nothing else, but somehow everything of His is so far away from me. I have not done anything very wicked, have I? But it isn't that . . . Go and get the pastor, I want him so much."

Niels rose and went for the pastor at once; he was grateful that this had not come at the very last moment.

The pastor came and was left alone with Gerda.

He was a handsome, middle-aged man with finely cut, regular features and large brown eyes. He knew, of course, Niels Lyhne's attitude to the church, and now and then some expressions of hostility that sprang from the young wife's fanaticism had been reported to him; but he never for a moment thought of speaking to her as to a heathen or an apostate, for he understood perfectly that it was only her love that had led her astray, and he also understood the feeling that impelled her, now that love could no longer follow her, to seek reconciliation with the God she had once known. Therefore he tried in his talk with her to wake her dormant memories by reading to her the passages from the Gospels and the hymns that he thought would be most familiar to her.

He was not mistaken.

The words woke intimate and solemn echoes in her soul like the pealing of bells on Christmas morning. Instantly there was spread before her eyes the land where our fancy is first of all at home, where Joseph dreamed and David sang, and where the leader stands that reaches from earth to heaven. It lay there with figs and mulberries, and the Jordan gleamed like clearest silver in the morning mist; Jerusalem stood red and somber under the setting sun; but over Bethlehem there was always glorious night with great stars in the deep blue vault. How her childhood faith welled up once more! She was again the little girl who went to church clinging to her mother's hand and sat there shivering with cold and wondering why people sinned so much. Then she grew to full stature again under the lofty words of the Sermon on the Mount, and she lay there like a prostrate sinner while the pastor spoke of the sacred mysteries of baptism and of holy communion. At last the true longing arose in her heart, the meek kneeling before the omnipotent and judging God, the bitter tears of remorse before the betrayed and reviled and tortured God, and the humbly audacious desire for the new covenant of wine and bread with the hidden God.

The pastor left her. Toward noon he came back and gave her the sacrament.

Her strength waned in a fitful flicker; yet at dusk, when Niels took her in his arms for the last time to say farewell before the shadows of death approached too near, she was fully conscious. But the love that had been the purest joy of his life died out of her eyes; she was no longer his; even now her wings were growing, and she yearned only for her God.

At midnight she died.

They were dreary months that followed. Time seemed to swell up into something enormous and hostile; every day was an unending desert of emptiness, every night a hell of memories. The summer was almost over before the rushing, frothing torrent of his grief had hollowed out a river bed in his soul where it could flow in a turgid, murmuring stream of sadness and longing.

Then it happened one day that he came home from the fields and found his little boy very ill. The child had been ailing for the last few days and had been restless in the night, but no one had believed it to be anything serious; now he lay in his little bed hot and cold with fever and moaning with pain.

The carriage was instantly sent to Varde for a physician, but none of the doctors were at home, and it had to wait for hours. At bedtime it had not yet returned.

Niels sat by the child's cot. Every half hour or oftener he would send someone out to listen and look for the carriage. A mounted messenger was also dispatched to meet it, but he failed to see any carriage and rode all the way to Varde.

This waiting for help that did not come made it all the more agonizing to watch the suffering of the sick child. The malady made rapid progress. Toward eleven the first attack of convulsions set in, and after that they came again and again at shorter and shorter intervals.

A little after one, the mounted messenger returned, saying that the carriage could not be expected for some hours yet, as none of the doctors had been at home when he rode out of town.

Then Niels broke down. He had fought against his despair as long as there was any hope, but now he could fight no more. He went into the dark parlor adjoining the sick room and stared out through the dusky panes, while his nails dug into the wood of the casement. His eyes seemed to burrow into the darkness for some hope; his brain crouched for a spring up toward a miracle; then suddenly all was still and clear for an instant, and in the clearness he turned away from the window to a table standing there, threw himself over it, and sobbed without tears.

When he came into the sick room again, the child was in convulsions. He looked at it as if he would stab himself to death with the sight: the tiny hands, clenched and white, with bluish nails, the staring eyes turning in their sockets, the distorted mouth, and the teeth grinding with a sound like iron on stone — it was terrible, and yet that was not the worst. No, but when the convulsions ceased and the body grew soft again, relaxing with the happy relief of lessened pain, then to see the terror that came into the child's eyes when it felt the first faint approach of the convulsions returning, the growing prayer for help when the pain came nearer and yet nearer — to see this and not be able to help, not with his heart's blood, not with all he possessed! He lifted his clenched hands threateningly to heaven, he caught up his child in a mad impulse of flight, and then threw himself down on the floor on his knees, praying to the Lord Who is in heaven, Who keeps the earth in fear through trials and chastisements, Who sends want and sickness, suffering and death, Who demands that every knee shall bend to Him in trembling, from Whom no flight is possible — either at the uttermost ends of the ocean or in the depths of the earth — He, the God Who, if it pleases Him, will tread the one you love best under His foot, torture him back into the dust from which He himself created him.

With such thoughts, Niels Lyhne sent prayers up to God; he threw himself down in utter abandonment before the heavenly throne, confessing that His was the power and His alone.

Still the child suffered.

Toward morning, when the old family physician drove in through the gate, Niels was alone.

Chapter XIV

*A*utumn had come; there were no flowers anymore on the graves up there in the churchyard, and the fallen leaves lay brown and moldering on the wet ground under the trees of Lönborggaard.

Niels Lyhne went about in the empty rooms in bitter despondency. Something had given way in him the night the child died. He had lost faith in himself, lost his belief in the power of human beings to bear the life they had to live. Existence had sprung a leak, and its contents were seeping out through all the cracks without plan or purpose.

It was of no avail that he called the prayer he had prayed a father's frenzied cry for help for his child, even though he knew none could hear his cry. He had known well what he did even in the depths of his despair. He had been tempted and had fallen; for it was a fall, a betrayal of himself and his ideal. No doubt tradition had been too strong in his blood. Humanity had cried to heaven in its agony for many thousands of years, and he had yielded to it, for he knew with the innermost fibers of his brain that gods were dreams, and he knew that when he threw himself into the arms of his fancies, that they *were* fancies. He had not been able to bear life as it was. He had taken part in the battle for the highest, and in the stress of the fight he had deserted the banner to which he had sworn allegiance; for after all, the new ideal, atheism, the sacred cause of truth — what did it all mean, what was it all but tinsel names for the one simple thing: to bear life as it was! To bear life as it was and allow life to shape itself according to its own laws!

It seemed to him as though his life had ended in that night of agony. What came after was no more than meaningless scenes tacked on after the fifth act when the action was already finished. He could, of course, take up his old principles again, if he felt so inclined, but he had once fallen the fall, and whether or not he would fall again mattered absolutely nothing.

This was the mood that possessed him most frequently.

Then came the November day when the King died, and war seemed more imminent.

He soon arranged his affairs in Lönborggaard and enlisted as a volunteer.

The monotony of training was easy to bear, for it seemed wonderful only to know that he was no longer superfluous, and when he was assigned to active service, the everlasting fight against cold, vermin, and discomforts of every kind drove his thoughts home and kept them from going farther afield than to what was right before his door. He grew almost cheerful over it, and his health, which had suffered under the griefs of the past year, was fully restored.

On a gloomy day in March he was shot in the chest.

Hjerrild, who was a physician in the hospital, had him put into a small room where there were only four beds. One of the men in there had been shot in the spine and lay quite still. Another was wounded in the breast and lay talking deliriously for hours at *a* time in quick, abrupt phrases. The third, who lay nearest Niels, was a great, strong peasant lad with fat, round cheeks; he had been struck in the brain by a fragment of a shell, and incessantly, hour after hour, about every half minute, he would lift his right arm and his right leg simultaneously and then let them fall again, accompanying his movements with a loud but dull and hollow "Hah-ho!" always in the same measure, always exactly the same, "Hah" when he lifted his limbs, "ho" when he let them fall.

There Niels Lyhne lay. The bullet had entered his right lung and had not come out again. In war not much circumlocution can be used, and he was told he had but little chance of life.

He was surprised; for he did not feel as though he were dying, and his wound did not pain him much. But soon a faintness came over him and warned him that the doctor was right.

So this was the end. He thought of Gerda, he thought of her constantly the first day, but he was always disturbed by the strange, cool look in her eyes the last time he had taken her in his arms. How beautiful it would have been, how poignantly beautiful, if she had clung to him to the very last and had sought his eye till her own was glazed in death; if she had been content to breathe out her life upon the heart that loved her so well instead of turning away from him at the last moment to save herself over into more life and yet more life!

On the second day in the hospital, Niels felt more and more oppressed by the heavy atmosphere in the room, and his longing for fresh air was strangely interwined in his mind with the desire to live. After all, there had been so much in life that was beautiful, he thought, as he remembered the fresh breeze along the shore at home, the cool soughing of the wind in the beech forests of Sjaslland, the pure mountain air of Clarens, and the evening zephyrs of Lake Garda. But when he began to think of human beings, his soul sickened again. He summoned them in review before him, one by one, and they all passed and left him alone, and not one stayed with him. But how far had he held fast to them? Had he been true? He had only been slower in letting go, that was all. No, it was *not* that. It was the dreary truth that a soul is always alone. Every belief in the fusing of soul with soul was a lie. Not your mother who took you on her lap, nor your friend, nor yet the wife who slept on your heart. . . .

Toward evening, inflammation set in, and the pain of his wound increased.

Hjerrild came and sat by him for a few minutes in the evening, and at midnight he returned and stayed a long time. Niels was suffering intensely and moaned with pain.

"A word in all seriousness, Lyhne," said Hjerrild. "Do you want to see a clergyman?"

"I have no more to do with clergymen than you have," Niels whispered angrily.

"Never mind me! I am alive and well. Don't lie there and torture yourself with your opinions. People who are about to die have no opinions, and those they have don't matter. Opinions are only to live by — in life they can do some good, but what does it matter whether you die with one opinion or another? See here, we all have bright, tender memories from our childhood; I have seen scores of people die, and it always comforts them to bring back those memories. Let us be honest! No matter what we call ourselves, we can never quite get that God out of heaven; our brain has fancied Him up there too often, the picture has been rung into it and sung into it from the time we were little children."

Niels nodded.

Hjerrild bent down to catch his words if he wished to say anything.

"You are very good," Niels whispered, "but" — and he shook his head decisively.

The room was still a long time except for the peasant lad's everlasting "Hah-ho!" hammering the hours to pieces.

Hjerrild rose. "Good-bye, Lyhne," he said. "After all, it is a noble death to die for our poor country."

"Yes," said Niels, "and yet this is not the way we dreamed of doing our part that time long, long ago."

Hjerrild left him. When he came into his own room, he stood a long while by the window looking up at the stars.

"If I were God," he said under his breath, and in his thoughts he continued, "I would much rather save the man who was converted at the last moment."

The pain in Niels's wound grew more and more intense; it tore and clutched at his breast, it persisted without mercy. What a relief it would have been if he had had a god to whom he could have moaned and prayed!

Toward morning he grew delirious, the inflammation was progressing rapidly.

So it went on for two more days and two more nights.

The last time Hjerrild saw Niels Lyhne he was babbling of his armor and of how he must die standing.

And at last he died the death — the difficult death.